Spicy Bites

Tattoo

2017

I0589130

ROMANCE
WRITERS
of Australia

Tattoo 2017: Spicy Bites Anthology

Anthology of Short Stories published by
Romance Writers of Australia Inc
© 2017

ebook format: 978-0-9577361-3-4
Print format: 978-0-9577361-2-2

Spicy Bites Coordinator: Tricia Sargant
Cover design by Lana Pecherczyk
Edited by Sarah Gates
Proofread by Claire Boston

Spicy Bites

Tattoo

Short Story Anthology
2017

Foreword

The word tattoo comes from the Polynesian word tatau, which means 'to write'. How perfect then is it that it is our theme for Romance Writers of Australia's first Spicy Bites Anthology!

Tattoos have been used over the centuries in various cultures across the world as talismans of protection, rites of passage, symbols of spiritual expression and religious devotion, marks of status and rank, decorations for bravery, marks of fertility, sexual lures and pledges of love. Negatively, they have been used as marks of slavery, outcasts and convicts; they've been used as punishment and have become a mark, for some, of horrific moments in our history.

In modern times, until recently, tattoos were associated with social outcasts, deviants, and criminals in Western society. However, this is changing and the tattoo is now becoming an expression of individuality, the skin a living canvas and the tattooists that ply their trade, artists in their own right. Tattoos can have a spiritual element for many, for others, they are a mark of belonging, creating a tie between people across cultures and within subcultures that at times, is stronger than blood.

It is for this reason that the tattoo was chosen as our theme for our first Spicy Bites Anthology. Like the tattoo, the more erotic side of literature has long been looked down upon, but like the tattoo, erotic stories are an expression of the human experience at its core, one of individuality, of spirituality and belonging.

It is my great pleasure in this last year as President of

Romance Writers of Australia, that I am able to bring the inaugural Spicy Bites: Tattoo Anthology to readers. In these pages you will find stories of romance, of exploration, of individuality and expression that all hold what is most important to the human condition at their core – being loved and belonging. Like a tattoo, I know they will be indelibly imprinted into your pleasure centres and bring you the dark, tantalising reads erotic stories are known for.

Enjoy!

Leisl Leighton
President RWA 2014-2017

Silver Linings
By
Nardia Sheriff

Tidy your desk.

Beth chuckled as the notification in the bottom right-hand corner of her screen faded. Old habits die hard, right? The last twenty minutes of a Friday afternoon had always been dedicated to a forensic desk clean. She couldn't help but line her red pens across the top of her keyboard, straighten her stationery and place her files neatly in her cabinets.

'What big, exciting plans do you have this weekend?' Jenny called from across her desk, knowing full well that any plans Beth had would hardly be big or exciting. Amused, Jenny continued, 'No, no. Don't tell me. You're having a steamy sex weekend with Sebastian Coleman.'

The snort escaped Beth before she could suppress it. Jenny's suggestion of a secret rendezvous with their hotter-than-Hades CEO was preposterous. She could count on one hand the times she'd come face-to-face with him in six years.

'You mock me now, Jenny, but one day I might just do something that will surprise you!'

Beth grinned, reflecting on her weekend plans. Feeling the blush make its way to her cheeks, she quickly lowered her face and made a show of capturing non-existent dust bunnies from behind her computer monitor. *Oh Lordy.* If only Jenny knew of her plans for the weekend. Sadly, they didn't include Sebastian Coleman—but they were certainly a far cry from the routine weekends she used to have.

'I won't hold my breath! Enjoy your rhumba, or whatever it is you do on a Friday night.' Jenny grabbed her handbag from the back of her chair, waved and headed for the door.

Reaching for her jacket, Beth glanced at the clock on the wall above the heads of her remaining colleagues. She needed to move if she wanted to get to Agent Provocateur before they closed at 5.30pm and squeeze in one final practice before her shift started at eight.

A zing of energy jolted through her at the thought of her upcoming shift. So much had changed in the year since Jason had walked out on her. Getting a second job had constituted a big change but as she reached over her shoulder to pat the freshly healed skin between her shoulder blades, she knew her metamorphosis was well underway. Change was a good thing. She might have something to thank Jason for after all.

Beth removed her hand and shrugged on her jacket. What was hidden there would make its debut outing tonight and she prayed that it would look as good in real life as she'd pictured in her head.

Flicking her short blonde bob over the jacket collar she grabbed her bag and made her way towards the elevators servicing the Coleman Corporation building. Her newfound confidence was testament to the fact her decision had been a good one. One fraught with risk, no doubt. *More like, risqué.* Beth smiled. *But what was it they said? With great risk comes great reward?*

As she waited for her ride, she turned to look over the sea of partitions across the floor.

'Have a fabulous weekend, peeps!'

Smiling, she noted the surprise on the faces of her workmates. She knew they thought she was a bit square; she was, after all, an accountant. But she no longer cared. It felt good to throw off old perceptions and push back against their expectations. With a wave, she stepped into the elevator and pressed the button that would take her to the bustling street and the little package that awaited her.

~ * ~

Seb Coleman loved his little brother. Of course he did. But there was a ten-year age gap between them and his little brother still had a lot of growing up to do. 'Fuck, Marcus we're already ten minutes late!'

Seb hated being late and, ever punctual, he detested the trait in others. 'The guys are outside waiting. We're gone if you don't get your arse down here in thirty seconds!'

Footsteps thundered down the stairs. 'Chill, bro, I'm here.'

The lack of urgency was evident as Marcus sauntered into the kitchen and although it irritated the shit out of Seb, he knew there was no point pressing the issue. As Best Man, he was supposed to be making sure the Buck had a great time—not ride his arse about time management.

Giving his big bro a shoulder barge, Marcus attempted to work out the plans for the evening. 'So where did you say we were going? Spearmint Rhino? Goldfingers?'

Seb stood from his stool, buttoned his suit jacket and motioned for Marcus to come closer. 'Curiosity killed the cat, little bro.' His fist connected playfully with Marcus' muscled bicep. 'You'll find out when we get there.'

He ushered his brother out onto the street where a Hummer limo stuffed full of Marcus' closest mates waited. 'Nice one, bro!' Marcus flashed Seb a massive grin before he was swamped in a sea of high fives and backslaps.

The kind of greeting reserved for the young and the clueless, Seb thought nostalgically. *C'mon old man, lighten up. Let the kid have his fun.* It was his brother's buck's night for Christ sake. Okay, so the Hummer wasn't his preference—but it was what Marcus wanted. Judging by the yahooing of boisterous lads, he'd hit the mark.

Seb sighed and corralled the men into the car. If it was up to him, they'd be on their way to his favourite whiskey bar. Marcus had quickly put the kibosh on those plans. Limo, booze and strippers in that order was the prerequisite, which made Seb wonder why Marcus bothered asking him at all.

He had, of course, obliged, but he'd avoided the trashy King Street clubs he knew Marcus would be expecting. Instead, he arranged a private room at the exclusive Masque. Not that he had any great aversion to strippers or booze as such. He had indulged in both in his time, but it now held little appeal. *Yep, officially an old man.*

A valet opened the door and Marcus' posse spilled out onto the sidewalk. Rounding up the crew, Seb pulled them into huddle formation.

'Here's to you Marcus. The last blowout before you head off into matrimonial bliss or whatever the hell she promised to get you to the altar.'

A chorus of macho cheers filled the crisp city air.

'Tonight is about you, but the tab is on me.' Amidst another round of cheering and backslapping they broke the huddle and piled through an oak door tucked into a stately brick building.

Seb brought up the rear. *Let the night begin, lads.*

~ * ~

Beth found the commotion of Masque's crowded dressing room intoxicating. Six months of watching scantily clad women clamouring for mirror space, plumping their cleavages and working magic with their make up brushes had taught her more about life than she'd thought possible. Beth shied away from the overt raunch-factor that featured in most of their performances, preferring to use raw sensuality through her dance as her point of difference.

Looking up from her mirror, Beth saw Sabrina, the manager, dispatching girls to their relevant performance areas. *Thank God for Sabrina!* Beth knew she was lucky. Given the exclusivity of Masque's clientele, it was her good fortune that Sabrina liked to mix up the entertainment at the club. She steered clear of the stereotypical troupe of blonde bimbos with big boobs, preferring to create a team of talented and physically diverse performers. It was what set Masque apart from the rest. Beth caught Sabrina's eye and smiled.

They had met through a dance class years before. In addition to keeping fit, Sabrina used the classes as a scouting ground for new talent. Beth had resisted Sabrina's recruitment attempts, until it became apparent that she needed some fast cash to buy out Jason's half of their home. Then it was Beth who'd cornered Sabrina and asked for the opportunity.

Now here she was. After her 'induction,' involving the

obligatory tits and arse, sequins and stilettos, in a group performance, Beth had finally graduated to a solo spot.

'You're up, Cat. Go make some money!' Sabrina gave her thumbs up.

Hearing her stage name snapped Beth back to the present and she gave herself the once over in the mirror. The soft gunmetal grey of the chiffon negligee she had picked up from Agent Provocateur fit her perfectly. The simplicity of the garment moulded to the curve of her hips and the swell of her full breasts with a hint of nipple under the sheer, floaty fabric. The boyleg panties in a matching grey satin were a far cry from the usual uniform of push up bras and g-strings. Twisting to view herself from behind, she reached over to smooth the little image situated between her shoulder blades and nodded. She was ready.

Time to knock 'em dead!

With five VIP rooms on her schedule that evening, she needed every tip she could earn and the better she performed, the bigger the tips. She felt fierce, sexy and powerful—a heady combination. Her luck was changing. Straightening her shoulders, Beth embraced her Cat persona and adjusted her silver ears and mask. *Fuck Jason for this past year of hell... But without it, I wouldn't have found me again.*

~ * ~

In spite of his early grumblings, Seb found himself enjoying the evening. Tightening his Zorro mask, he felt himself loosen up after his fifth drink and was now happy to sit back in the studded leather club chair and soak up the antics of his younger brother doing shots with his mates.

Although Masque was a classier establishment than most, the reality was that gorgeous women with huge boobs and tight arses were the staple of strip clubs the world over. *So just enjoy it for what it is.*

'Now, we know that you've got a soft spot for all things pussy, gentlemen,' a sultry, disembodied voice emanated from behind the curtain, eliciting whoops and cheers as the bucks jockeyed for the best viewing position around the stage.

'But not all cats are claws and spitfire,' the throaty voice continued. 'Sometimes, an exotic Siamese or Abyssinian will catch your eye, captivating you with her elegance and grace… much like our enchanting Cat.' A collective growl rumbled through the crowd as the voice dissipated.

The stage suddenly lit up in bright white light and at the centre stood a lone figure, bathed in white rays.

The sheer grey lingerie, cut exquisitely low at the back caught Seb's eye, but it was a small mark between the curves of her shoulder blades that had him moving to a seat closer to the stage. *A tattoo?* Many of the dancers had tattoos but the calm and ethereal vibe Cat emitted had him straining for a closer look.

He was met with two dark eyes and a smiling mouth full of teeth, etched in ink, staring back at him.

Curious. Seb sat back, fixated.

The music began. Cat arched her back and did a slow, languid backflip before effortlessly dropping to the floor. Using her whole body, she contorted herself in a twisting move that saw her back on her feet before Seb even realised she was standing. *So graceful and fluid, she'd be like melting into a bed of silk.* Fleeting surprise registered at the thought before his attention was drawn back to the movement on the stage. He was staring. He couldn't remember the last time he'd simply stared at a woman.

Somewhere in the fog that was his brain, Seb recognised the acoustic music but he couldn't pick it. He didn't care. Tearing his eyes from her to check on Marcus' entourage, he could see that they weren't immune to the spell that Cat was weaving either. The dark flimsy material swirled as she danced a hypnotic path. Glimpses of curves and mounds greeted them with every twist and tumble she executed. It was one of the sexiest things Seb had ever seen. It was entirely different from the girls they'd been watching earlier that evening. Seb felt like a voyeur, peeking into Cat's bedroom window.

Low, sultry words crooned through invisible speakers. *The world was on fire but no one could save me but you…*

If it wasn't on fire, it was certainly beginning to smoulder. Seb shifted in his seat; there was only one cause of his discomfort and she was spinning her seductive web in front of him.

~ * ~

With the stage lights beaming, Beth couldn't see more than a few shadows as she glanced at her audience. She knew that it was a buck's night with around a dozen young men and an open chequebook. Most of the VIP room bookings were buck's nights. Provided they were forthcoming with the tips, Beth didn't really care who they were. As the first chorus ended, she focused on her routine; the big reveal was only moments away. She had worked hard at pouring as much angst and emotion into the dance as she could. The exhilaration of her first solo performance, in spite of the shitstorm that was at its origin, had Beth feeling invincible.

She had put her dreams of being a professional dancer on hold to attend university, knowing it was what her parents wanted. But it was dancing, and these men with their chequebooks, who would get her out of the mess Jason had created.

As the second verse began, the lights dimmed. The slow rhythmic dance had been choreographed to seduce, to hypnotise using the rich bass beat pulsing into every corner of the room and into the core of every man seated there, watching her. And now that she had every eye in the room trained on her dancing form, it was time. *Showtime.*

~ * ~

Seb had seen many performances at Masque, entertaining his American clients. He'd seen dancers with snakes, exotic costumes and impressive acrobatics. But as sure as fuck, he had never been left breathless and throbbing after watching one. The tightness in his trousers was matched by the stiffness in his shoulders from leaning forward, intent in his viewing. He'd never seen anything as sensual or erotic as the woman up on stage.

The bright white of the lights dimmed and Cat stopped in the centre of the stage, looking out at the crowd. Seb willed her to look at him as she scanned the room. The strain in his pants was unrelenting and as his upper body coiled tighter he prayed she would stop. When the silver mask turned and her eyes landed on him, he was a goner. She'd chosen him and her eyes bore into his. Energy flared and arced as Seb lost all concept of time and place. His poker face was lacking, even the strip of black fabric that covered half of his face could not mask his raw desire. He wanted her. He desired her. *Fuck*. He was in trouble.

She gave an imperceptible nod and turned away from him to face the back of the stage; her head hung low exposing her milky white back. The smile inked between her shoulder blades mocked him. *She's got your number pal. You're toast.*

As the lights faded to black, Seb's heart rate tripled. She was gone. The whole room plunged into darkness. *That can't be it!* He stifled a moan of relief as the soft purple hue of an ultraviolet light bathed her silhouette, revealing she hadn't moved an inch. But something had changed. Slowly, a bright neon glow illuminated her alabaster skin.

Bolting to his feet, Seb grimaced as the sudden movement threatened to expose just how close he was to losing control, but he had to get closer. Stepping towards the stage, an image on Cat's back materialised. He was standing at the edge of the stage like a kid at a Wiggles concert, before he realised her tattoo had become a cat. *The Cheshire Cat.*

The distinctive grinning face made much more sense now as the stripes of the cat's round body and its sphinx-like pose became clear.

'I'll be damned.'

~ * ~

Every fibre of her being was pinging by the time she returned to the dressing room. She knew she'd nailed her performance, but the awakening of her libido, currently emitting little zaps of energy that caused her body to hum, was a whole new level of surprise. Beth welcomed the zing that was causing her to clench in places that had been lying dormant for some time.

'Oh my God, that was perfect!' Sabrina enveloped her in a hug.

Beth was grateful for the exuberant greeting. Not only was she relieved her first performance was over, but she needed some time to process what had just happened. She knew he couldn't have recognised her. *Not a chance.* But when the lights had dimmed and she'd scanned the room, she'd recognised him instantly—even with the mask. Sebastian Coleman. Unable to look away, their eyes had locked. She had forced herself to turn around, but not before she saw what was written all over his face. There was no mistaking his desire. *He wanted her!*

The fluttering card hit Beth on the forehead before she realised Crystal was even talking to her.

'You got yourself an admirer, Newbie. Dunno what he sees in you but he just gave me a thousand bucks to give you his number.' Turning on her six-inch heels, Crystal tottered back into the lounge to collect her delivery fee.

Beth knew it was from him before she'd even read it. Her insides flipped between wanting to launch into a full-blown panic and seeing an irresistible opportunity emerge. Her thighs tightened as heat began to pool low in her belly. The need for panic vanished as she let the seed that had been planted flourish. She read the card.

'Jesus, Mary and Joseph!' Beth buried her face in her hands and tried to suppress the throbbing that was consuming her. If scribbles on the back of a business card brought her to this, she could only imagine what being with him would elicit. *Decision made.* She was going to meet him.

'You okay?' Sabrina tapped Beth on the shoulder, startling her back into the reality of preparing for her next performance.

'Uh, huh.' Beth grinned to reinforce the white lie. 'Still riding the high.'

Oblivious to her inner turmoil, Sabrina nodded. 'You should be Beth. The tips you're raking in... Wow! One of those guys just dropped five grand on you—plus smaller tips for the other girls. You're a rising star and the gamble paid off, my friend. Who knew a UV tattoo could be so sexy?'

The power radiating from her was exhilarating. Pulling on her mask and straightening her ears, Beth practically floated to the stage door.

Ka-ching!

~ * ~

Even hunched over a drink at the bar, he cut an impressive

figure. With her shift finished, it didn't take long for Beth to spot him amongst the stragglers. *He'd waited.* He was nursing a scotch on the rocks, staring mindlessly in front of him. There was no sign of his entourage. Beth assumed they'd been sent to the next club without him.

She hadn't responded to his message, deciding to make him wait. If he wanted her, he needed to work for it. Glad she decided to stay in her negligee, Beth took a deep breath. She'd thrown her jacket over the top to keep her relative modesty intact, but there was no denying the sheer lingerie made her feel invincible. She needed all the courage she could get to face Sebastian Coleman. *The time for waiting is over.*

'Can I get you another drink, sir?'

Seb spun around to face the voice behind him.

'Ah, Cheshire Cat. You came.'

'It was an invitation I couldn't refuse.'

Beth looked for a sign that he'd recognised her but saw none. His mask was still in place, but then so was hers; Masque house rules still applied. Seb noticed too.

'Two masked figures meet.'

His fingers tweaked the cat ears perched in her hair and trailed a finger along her mask and down her jawline. Beth didn't pull away. She took a step closer.

'Indeed we do.'

The flame that had been smouldering hours earlier reignited, scorching her from the inside. Reaching to steady herself, she placed a hand on his shoulder and stared. Just because she'd drawn the line at turning tricks in her newfound career, didn't mean she couldn't exercise her own right to casual sex. She needed this. Not just to exorcise old ghosts, but for her. *And the chance of some really hot, orgasmic sex.*

Beth's eyes gleamed as she held Seb's gaze.

Emboldened by the desire she saw there, she took the opportunity to step further into the space between his thighs, tracing feathery trails towards his obvious bulge.

'Did your tailor not measure you correctly?' She flicked a finger across the straining zipper.

Seb reached for her hand and pressed it hard against his cock so there was no mistaking his intent.

'And here I was thinking you were a good girl.'

Leaning forward, her lips resting against his cheek, Beth gave a squeeze from under his hand, smoothing her thumb along the ridge there and whispered. 'Appearances are deceiving, Mr Coleman. Now get me out of here before I fuck you, right here on this bar stool.'

Seb needed no further invitation. Beth waited until they had turned into the darkened laneway leading towards his hotel before blocking his path.

Relishing in the unfamiliar situation and invigorated by her power, she leaned against his broad chest and breathed him in before hooking a hand behind his neck, tugging him closer and covering his mouth with her own. *No turning back now.*

A primal grunt escaped Seb's lips as she staked her claim and propelled them back towards a dark corner. She didn't care they were still in the laneway. All she knew is she needed Seb inside her now or she was going to die.

To quell the ache that was spreading like wildfire through her body. She needed him to make love to her. *No, fuck her!*

'You need to fuck me. Now.' She reached for his trousers, heady with anticipation.

'I'll get that,' Seb growled.

Stepping back, Beth created some space between them. *He needs this too.* She didn't care why. She only cared that he was going to fuck her. Belt flung aside and zipper gaping, Beth closed the gap between them. She pressed her hips against an impressive erection that jerked in response, itching to fully escape its tight restraints.

Her hands were on him before he had even pushed his boxers away. As her lips captured his again, she slid a hand between their hips, cupping his balls and giving them a slight squeeze before encasing his cock in her palm.

'Do that again and it's all over, Cat.' Spinning them both around, Seb pushed her against the rough bricks.

Moving his hand beneath her jacket, Seb sought out the sensitive nub hidden within the shroud of grey satin. Convulsions rippled through her body as he found what he was looking for and rolled her clit between his thumb and forefinger. Beth hung onto his shoulders for dear life. As she rode his hand, she edged closer and closer to oblivion. Seb broke contact, bringing the fingers that had been working their magic from underneath her coat. Beth whimpered. With her eyes fixed on his, she watched as Seb lifted his fingertips, still slick with her juices and bought them to his lips. He sucked.

Sucker punched, Beth gasped for air. 'Enough, Seb. Now!'

Cool air sliced between them as Seb leaned back to pull a foil package from inside his jacket. *Protection!* As he turned his attention to the task, Beth gave silent thanks for his gentlemanly gesture. *She hadn't even given it a thought.* Then all thought was gone. Making light work of her panties, Seb wrapped her leg around his hip, angled himself and in a single stroke drove deep into her.

He was relentless and Beth revelled in it. It was rough and gritty, primal and base. She was being fucked. And she loved it. She wanted more.

Nipping at his ear, she urged him to fuck her harder, deeper. Wrapping her other leg around his waist, she used the wall behind her as leverage and drilled him back. Grinding his hips against hers, Seb groaned. It was all the permission Beth needed. Anchored against the wall, Beth gave in to the exquisite sensations consuming her. A sob escaped her lips as her orgasm ripped her apart. She might die after all. Seb's grip on her hips tightened as shudders wracked his body. Pounding her against the rough bricks one last time, he buried his face into her shoulder before letting loose a muffled roar.

Beth leaned back against the wall with Seb's head resting on her collarbone, her senses alive in wonderment. 'Intriguing, Mr Coleman. You do know what they say about curiosity though, don't you?'

Seb could barely swallow. Of all the scenarios, of all the ways, he never anticipated the most mind-blowing sex of his life would be had in a back alley tucked away between a fire escape and a dump. It felt so seedy, but perfectly awesome.

He sucked in a breath. Without attempting to remove himself from inside her, he replied, 'Something about killing the cat? Trust me Cat, that's the last thing I want to do to you.'

'On the contrary, sir, I want you to kill me. Torture me with your body. Annihilate me with your mouth. Another seven times over, please?' Beth moved her hips suggestively. She reached up and removed Seb's mask. 'But, I need to save my ninth life for my next shift. Just so you know.'

~ * ~

Finance Presentation – 15 minutes

Beth pressed snooze on the reminder flashing in the corner of her screen. She picked up her stack of reports and went to prepare the conference room for the presentation she had, up until recently, been dreading. Not anymore. After the weekend she'd just had, anything the quarterly Finance Committee threw at her would be a walk in the park. *Thank God Sebastian doesn't attend these meetings.*

Beth oozed confidence. Jenny had commented on how self-assured she appeared that morning. And she was—she was fearless. Fucking Seb was only a part of it. Decisions *she* had made, risks *she* had taken were the reason she was walking on cloud nine.

Making her way around the large walnut conference table, Beth distributed a bundle of reports at each seat and then set about ensuring the projector was working properly. Checking the power connections under the table, she noticed the laptop wasn't plugged in. *Damn.* Crawling under the table in a pencil skirt and a silk blouse wasn't ideal but she didn't have time to call IT. Kicking off her shoes, she climbed under.

Sorted.

Unperturbed by the sound of the door opening, Beth crawled out from under the table, catching the collar of her silk shirt on an armrest.

'I'm down here, Peter, but I'm stuck.'

Two trouser clad legs blocked her path.

'Curiouser and curiouser.'

Beth froze. *Surely not?* 'Peter? C'mon, help me unhook my blouse so I can get up.'

'No.'

The pause lasted forever.

'I was looking for Peter. I wasn't expecting this.' Fingertips touched the skin between her shoulder blades, exposed by the caught shirt. Slowly tracing an outline around two round eyes, and a full, toothy grin.

'I never got the opportunity to ask you, why a Cheshire Cat?' Seb reached down to release Beth and helped her to her feet.

'If you don't know where you are going, any road will get you there,' she whispered, quoting the Lewis Carroll classic.

'I have no idea what that even means, and I don't care.' Lifting her chin, Seb forced Beth to look at him before crushing his lips against her own. A herd of stampeding buffalo had nothing on the hammering of her heart as she sunk into his embrace. It was like coming home.

'You work for me.' It was more of a statement than a question. His lips broke contact giving Beth the chance to think clearly again.

Not wanting to step away, she murmured, 'Ever since I graduated.'

'That night, you left and didn't leave a note, a number... anything. Like it meant nothing.' Seb's voice conveyed his hurt.

'I work for you Sebastian! It's complicated.' Beth stepped backwards to escape his embrace but Seb held her firm. Looking over his shoulder, Beth could see the heads of various managers bobbing behind frosted glass, on their way into the conference room.

'They're coming!' Breaking free from his grasp, Beth smoothed over her skirt and straightened her blouse. She moved towards her seat but not before Seb reached out and smoothed down a strand of flyaway hair.

'We need to talk. In my office, after this meeting.' The look in Seb's eyes made it clear what would happen when they met in his office—and talking was an unlikely scenario.

As the door opened, Seb let her go, turning to address the assembling team. 'I'm stepping in for Craig today. He's ill.' The managers settled into their seats as Seb turned to Beth.

He nodded to her. 'Now that we've met properly, please begin. I look forward to watching you perform today.'

The Tattooed Heart
By
Audrey Fraser

Lila had a secret.

It was a secret she kept extremely quiet. She told no one. And yet, thousands knew. Of course, those thousands didn't know her real name. To them, she was simply Corazon—the sultry voiced female on AudioErotic, weaving tales of explicit debauchery with the mysterious Him.

Corazon was a vixen, teasing anonymous online users with only her voice. She recorded herself, describing her most wanton fantasies and sent them out into cyberspace. What her listeners didn't know was that the man described in her little stories was real. That was a secret so tightly kept that even *he* didn't know about it. Never referred to by name, the stories she wove were fantasies she'd had about her hot housemate. Matt.

It had come about when the mining boom had struck again. Lila had a good job, but it didn't extend to allowing for the rise in her rent. Prices for everything had skyrocketed and while Lila loved living on her own, she just couldn't wear the correspondingly high rent increase. Advertising for a housemate had been the solution to a crappy situation. Mind you, she never expected someone like Matt to rock up on her doorstep.

They had spoken on the phone and everything she'd asked him had checked out, and while his voice had definitely been on the roughened, knicker-melting side, she didn't get her hopes up for when he arrived. That had been a mistake, because the

15

contrast of his voice and what she'd imagined him to actually look like had been all the more jarring when she flung open the door... and there he was.

He had hair clipped close to the scalp and a light beard that until that very moment, Lila could've sworn didn't turn her on in the least. He was a handsome devil and a card-carrying gentleman, which was proven when she attempted to help him move in and was kindly told that he didn't want to bother her—and did she want him to cook tonight, since she was letting him stay?

It had been lucky that she'd had the wall behind her to keep her upright. The combination of the courtesy, the offer and the cheeky grin as he walked his very fine backside into the house had Lila's knees dangerously weak. She obligingly let him get settled in, then took herself to her own room to very quietly finger-fuck herself to orgasm.

The man was a god in the kitchen and Lila considered it a fair trade when she offered to do the dishes that he hated. That evening, after what Lila called a sumptuous dinner, but Matt shrugged off as 'just basics,' was the beginning of her very hot, very explicit dreams about the cute guy who'd just moved in. It was the start of her rampant fantasies about Matt, the things she would do to him, the things she would want him to do to her. But somehow, she never got the opportunity to test the waters with him and before she knew it, the time to spring such an idea on him had passed. Accidentally, she'd become friends with the hot guy living in her spare room.

There was no vent for her frustration and her vibrator was on constant recharge. If she wasn't careful, she'd wear it out. She'd inadvertently found a pressure valve for her hot little daydreams when she started recording her fantasies as an audio file. Then, the real 'fuck it' moment came when she uploaded them onto the internet. Submitting that first file anonymously as Corazon had given her a thrill the likes of which she hadn't ever experienced. To her utter shock, the listeners who had heard the sample bought the digital copy and clamoured for more.

Lila obliged.

Each explicit daydream she had was recorded and uploaded for the voracious sexual appetites of her listening audience. Lila vented her feelings with explicit, naughty audio recordings, available to anyone who subscribed to the AudioErotic site. It was addictive and gloriously freeing, but something she could never, ever tell anyone. Especially not the object of all her lusty flights of imagination.

It got to a point where the revenue from her little 'side-job' afforded her a little breathing room, financially. She had contemplated having her flat to herself again but... there were so many reasons not to. Apart from the weird comfort having another human being in the house provided, Matt was an excellent cook, a great housemate and she wouldn't dare leave him to the tender mercies of a rampant rental market. She did celebrate her unexpected windfall, however, with a secret desire she'd had for a while. She'd gotten herself a tattoo. It was a small, simple, delicate design, not much more than a black line of ink. And she knew exactly where she wanted it.

The guy—Jordan—had looked at the design, looked at her and smirked a little.

'You want this on your wrist?'

'Nope,' she said cheerfully and was gratified to see his eyes widen for a fraction of a second when Lila informed him that the tattoo was going somewhere far more... intimate. That tiny heart was going on the crease of her hip, just below the bone. Only the most privileged of people would ever see it, and the naughty buzz she got knowing of her little secret was something to bolster her on less-than-stellar days.

It didn't take long, but still, Lila was squirming by the time Jordan had finished with her. Reclining on that sterile, plastic covered chair, with that man's head hovering so close, just above her groin, instantly made her damp beneath her undies.

'Hold still,' he muttered, as the tattoo gun bit into her flesh. It was like raking fingernails across sun-burned skin. The icy cold wipes he used to clean the blood and excess ink away only heightened the sensation in her lap, it was all she could do not to buck up against the strength of his hands holding her gently in place. She was a little embarrassed, even though they were screened from view.

Sitting there in nothing more than her t-shirt and knickers, with his hands splayed over her hips, her arousal surfaced despite the burn and bite of the needle. She could feel his warm breath sweeping across her sensitised skin, her nipples were hard and if he looked up, he'd be able to see the points of them pressing against her shirt. It had been a while since she'd had a man's hands caressing her skin—even if it was to permanently mark it.

Tipping her head back and staring at the ceiling, her mind's eye took her into that orgasmic land of daydream where another man's head hovered tantalisingly over her slick, wet pussy. In this fantasy, Matt was tattooing her, but had taken up a position between her legs, as opposed to her side where the real-life Jordan was working. Dream-Matt would glance up wickedly from where he was 'for better positioning.' Or so he would tell her.

Lila amused herself with an imaginary Matt setting aside the tattoo gun to slide her underwear off her with his teeth, using that clever tongue on her labia and flicking it up across her clit, sucking and nibbling and thoroughly enjoying himself as she edged closer to climax. All this while Jordan inked the sweetly delicate little heart underneath her hipbone.

The tattoo was done long before Lila had finished with her fantasy. Jordan had obviously been able to smell her arousal drifting up from her overheated sex, as he gave her a business card and urged her to come back if she ever needed another tattoo done, ever again. No really, *anytime*. She'd smiled sweetly, taken the card, and gone home to finish in peace.

~ * ~

Lila bounced down the stairs, her tattoo healed nicely under her clothes, hoping to convince Matt to cook her breakfast. She wanted him to make *her* breakfast, but even Lila knew how far-fetched that was going to be. She skidded to a halt in the doorway of her kitchen to the mouth-watering sight of Matt, leaning over the kitchen counter, propped on elbows, reading the newspaper. He was wearing nothing except pyjama bottoms and a lot of mouth-watering skin.

Bouncing one hip and bobbing his head to the music playing from his phone, which was docked to a small speaker in the kitchen, Lila managed to recover her wits and cheerily greet him.

The image of that undulating bum of his was going straight into her fantasy folder.

'Any chance of brekkie this morning?' she asked him, mentally filing away the tempo of his hip thrusts to add to her imaginations later.

'Fair to mid.' He grinned, pushing himself up. 'How would you like some coffee to start with, and while you're sipping that, you can tell me all about your latest exploits?'

Lila nearly choked. How did he know about her most recent—and extremely vivid—dream about him? Oh god, did she talk in her sleep? Was her wet dream so intense she *actually screamed out his name*?

'Exploits?' she squeaked. Matt looked back at her enquiringly.

'Yeah. We haven't really caught up for a couple days. How's work been? Did the transfer go over a bit smoother than you thought it would? I know you were stressing about that.'

Holy shit. Work. He meant *work* exploits. The relief she felt must been on her face because his affable smile widened into a teasing grin.

'Ohhh, what did you *think* I meant? Why, naughty Miss Lila, what have you been doing?'

Lila blushed, but, mercifully, he let the matter drop and nodded to his phone still in the dock.

'Do me a favour and put something else on, would you? That playlist is nearly over.'

Hopping onto the kitchen bench in order to reach the dock where he'd stashed it—honestly, it was like he forgot how long his arms were—she started scrolling through his music files.

'No Bieber though, okay?' he said. 'Can't stand the guy.'

'You have Justin Bieber on your phone?' Lila said with interest. He shot her a warning look over his shoulder that had her crossing her legs.

'I don't. But I figure you'll probably rectify that.'

Lila snorted. 'No fear! Don't care for the pre-pubescent child myself. You're safe.'

He visibly relaxed as he turned back to the coffee maker, though she did make plans to download every single one of Katy Perry's songs onto his phone and set it to random. Having

'I Kissed a Girl' blasting out in between his heavy metal numbers would be priceless. Especially if he happened to be at work.

Swiping her finger upward, looking through his enormous collection of songs, Lila's heart faltered in her chest as she told herself there was no way—*no way in hell*—that what she saw was possible. Slowly retracing her way back in the list, she paused, barely breathing as she read, then re-read what simply couldn't be true.

Corazon.

For three solid seconds, she stared in utter shock at the tiny screen. Then, while a twist of mortification had unfurled in her belly, a stronger and more powerful emotion swamped it. *Intrigue.*

Matt *listened* to her. He listened to *her* voice as she described the wicked, dirty things she would have liked to do to and with him. Her gaze slid across to where he fussed with the machine. Did he know? Did he at least suspect? How was it possible that he didn't recognise her voice? Although... now that she thought about it, the voice she used on her recordings was low and sexy, slightly muffled through the microphone and reminiscent of Jessica Rabbit. Not her usual voice at all. It was entirely possible that the man simply hadn't seen what was right in front of his eyes the whole time.

Lila stared down at phone for a heartbeat longer and made a decision that was possibly the riskiest she'd ever make in her whole life. She randomly flicked the screen and pressed play on whatever it landed upon. Van Halen started wailing, 'I got Elvis on my elbow.'

'Nice!' Matt said as he immediately started to shake his hips to the rock song blasting from the small speakers. She turned the volume down so that their neighbours wouldn't have any reason to complain this early on a Saturday morning. Matt kept bumping and thrusting around the kitchen.

She waited until he was reaching into the fridge for the milk—note to self, get more *milk and juice*—and slid off the bench.

'Hey, Matt?'

'Hmm?' He was pouring the milk for frothing and wasn't

paying attention when she slid her arms around him from behind.

'You okay sunshine?' he asked as he set the milk down, she could hear the concern in his tone and her skin prickled as he ran his hands over hers where they were clasped over his belly.

'I'm fine,' she managed to say without too much of her nerves creeping into her voice, 'It's just... Look, I want to tell you something, okay?'

'Sure.'

'It's something I've never told anyone before.' Her cheek pressed to the smooth, warm skin of his back. She felt him still, the muscles stretching as he twisted vainly to see her over his shoulder.

'Okay, Lila.'

She gave his gut a squeeze and he grunted. 'I mean it Matt, I've never told this to anyone before. No one. I'm trusting you with this.'

'You've got it. Nothing goes past us.'

She hesitated, feeling her heartbeat thundering in her chest as she was about to take the first step into what would either be the best, or possibly *worst*, decision of her life. Her cheek was still pressed to his skin and his hand brushed against her thigh. They stayed there, just breathing slowly in and out on a lazy Saturday morning. She rocked her hips forward the tiniest little bit, without even thinking, he really did have the most delectable arse. She blew out a breath and began.

'I've got this secret,' she started, allowing her body to relax a little as she cuddled up to Matt, inhaling the mingling scents of his freshly showered body and the brewing coffee. He made a non-committal noise that indicated he was listening, without interrupting.

'You see, there's this guy I know. He's one of the greatest people I've ever met, and I think he's really hot.'

As she spoke, her voice slowly slid into her Jessica Rabbit persona. Low and sultry, a languid, sexy voice. She could tell when it began to register. He hadn't figured it out just yet, but... he recognised the voice from somewhere else and couldn't quite place it.

'I've been having the hottest dreams about him; god, he

makes me so horny! Thoughts about him distract me at the most random times of day. I could be grocery shopping and think "I really want Him to drag that slice of fruit over my skin before licking the juice off and fucking me senseless".'

Now she had him. More than just her words, which painted a fresh image of them fucking each other in her mind—she knew the instant he had recognised Corazon's voice coming out her, Lila's, mouth. His hand stilled completely and she felt the jerk of realisation. He didn't move away. In fact, his hands clamped down on hers, as if daring her to even try to tug away. She flexed her fingertips, just enough to lightly scrape across the soft skin of his belly and Matt sucked in a sharp breath before it shuddered out.

'He was the most attractive man I'd seen in a long time, and I wanted him from almost the moment I saw him. You see, he won me over not just by being sexy as hell, but by being this genuinely terrific guy... He cooks like a dream too.'

Matt chuckled, but she could hear the breathy strain in the texture of it. She stretched up on her toes, noting that her nipples had tightened and hardened and there was no way he could possibly miss the way they dragged against the skin of his back, even through her shirt. A puff of her breath tickled his ear as she whispered, 'You know, I had to make myself come within minutes of meeting him. He's that potent.'

Daring to nip at that earlobe, she sank back down and placed a sweet little kiss beneath a shoulder blade. She rocked her hips against him with a touch more pressure this time.

'The thing is, this guy, he's completely oblivious to me. I would have to do something completely outrageous to get his attention. It could go so horribly wrong, Matt. He's one of my best friends, but if I don't fuck him, and fuck him soon...' This was accompanied by another unmistakable hip roll and a stronger flexing of fingernails against his abs that made the muscles under her fingers jump reflexively. 'I'm going to burn out another vibrator, or go up in flames myself.'

Emboldened by the fact that he hadn't thrust her away in disgust, in fact, if she were perfectly honest, she would say that he was rolling his own hips in the most miniscule undulations. He was turned on. By *her*. His heart thundered, his breath rasped in and out in a most gratifying way. Lila found the courage to edge her finger tips down past the waistband of his pyjama bottoms. She stilled, fingertips barely underneath the elastic, giving him a chance to back out of this, to recoil in horror ... but he didn't. Her smile curved saucily against his warm skin and she reached just a little further past the waistband of his pants. She stretched on her toes again, dragging her nipples up his back more purposefully and throatily whispered against his ear.

'Do you want me?' she asked, nipping the earlobe, a fierce shiver raking its way down his body. His only sound was an unintelligible groan.

'Is that a yes, Matt? Because if it isn't, we can stop right now.'

Her hands didn't even have time to move away from his skin entirely before his hands were gripped over hers.

'*Yes.*'

His voice was hoarse and rough and it emboldened her to take the plunge and wrap her hands around the stiff length of his cock. Her fingers held the thick, hard cock she had fantasised about for months. She was going to *enjoy* this. Her hand gripped him as she slowly slid her curled palm up and down his shaft.

'Is this what it's like when you listen to my audios, Matt? Does it get this hard? This fast?' She released her grip for a nanosecond, before squeezing him gently at the base of his cock, eliciting a heartfelt groan and terse word to fall from his lips as he collapsed forward a little. His hands braced against the kitchen bench as he breathed hard. Pre-cum had coated the head of his dick. She slid her hand up and down the shaft faster as her own arousal grew.

'Do you stroke yourself late at night, in bed, listening to my voice? Did you like to play hard with yourself?' She jerked several times in a flurry of movement that dragged a whimper from his lips. 'Or did you like it slow, easy, so the climax sneaks up on you and takes you by surprise?'

She gentled her hand accordingly and was appreciative of the low growl in the back of his throat.

'Which way did you like best, Matt?' she allowed herself a

low, dirty chuckle before grazing her teeth over the cord of muscle at the top of his shoulder. 'I think your favourites were the rough ones, the filthy ones. The stories where we just fuck wherever we happen to be.'

He reached down and wrapped his hand over hers, guiding her the way he liked it best. More than the languid caress she had indulged in, mostly for her own pleasure, but less than the almost violent stroking a few moments ago.

'Did you ever think about what she would look like Matt? Corazon. Did you ever pretend she was me? That it was my body your hands were on? That it was my mouth on you, my pussy you fucked?'

He was gasping for breath now, but he managed to nod. Lila nearly froze, but let her hands do the talking, so to speak, when she gripped his cock a little firmer and gave him a long, sensuous stroke.

'Then I must confess Matt. Every single one of my audio files? Every story I told. In every one of them, I was thinking about you.'

'Oh *fuck*.'

Matt spun, his cock wrenching out of her grasp. He wrapped his arms around her in the next moment, his mouth crashing down on hers passionately. He nipped and sucked on her lips, his tongue delving into her mouth and thrusting. It was without doubt, the dirtiest kiss she'd ever experienced, and she could feel the warm slick sensation between her thighs. She could come just from the kiss if she could get enough of it. She must have mewled, or made some noise, because she felt his mouth curl into a self-satisfied smirk.

'I've been wanting to do that for months.'

'What took you so long?' she asked breathlessly as he took the opportunity to yank her pyjama top up and off, over her head. Later they would find it dangling from the light fitting. But in this moment, Matt's eyes were fixated on her breasts, the nipples tight under the almost physical caress of his gaze.

'I was trying to be a gentleman.'

His hands drifted up to cup her breasts experimentally, his thumbs flicking over the tight nipples. Lila let her head drop back as the man of her fantasies explored her body after months of anticipation.

'You've been driving me insane,' he muttered.

'Who? Me? Or Corazon?'

'Both of you!' The glower he shot her only caused her to grin.

'You started this sweetheart,' she taunted him. 'You're the one who waltzed in here with that sexy arse and turned me on in seconds.'

He stared at her for a second and recognition flared in the depths of his eyes. 'The Visitor,' he breathed. Lila nodded.

'That was about our first encounter. Or rather, what I wish had happened.'

His hands hadn't stopped roaming her body, so she missed the sensation the moment he stilled and looked her directly in the eye.

'I'm going to fuck you,' he said in a tone that dared her to disagree. His eyes fell to the round swells of her breasts, tipped with those aching, rosy nipples.

Lila only nodded. 'Okay.'

'I don't think you understand, Lila.' His eyes lifted and she was struck by the intensity and seriousness in his gaze. This was a man who finally had his goal within reach and would let nothing stop him.

'I'm going to fuck you every single way that you described. Until you've screamed out my name—not some anonymous online listener. Until your legs are water and we've pissed off the neighbours.'

He leaned in close—close enough that she had to lean back against the kitchen counter to see his eyes—and his erection pressed hard against her. The only thing between them was her thin, soaked cotton knickers.

'Until you make that sound when you orgasm. Until I've made you come so hard you forget your own name for a moment.'

Hands under her arms he lifted her effortlessly onto the counter, nudging her legs apart so he could step between them. She matched his height this way and he took advantage, kissing her again. There was less intensity this time, but the passion underneath remained. He nipped and suckled his way across her jaw and down her neck, lingering on her clavicle, before wrapping his lips around one hard, pointing nipple. Lila gasped at the sensation, the suction and sharp nip of teeth, swiftly soothed away with a swirl of tongue. Her fingers gripped his hair. She loved that he couldn't keep his hands, lips, or anything else, off her.

She'd been so thoroughly distracted by the marvellous things he was doing with his tongue that she startled when he fisted his hand around the snug fabric of her knickers and ripped them right off. She gasped in shock and then laughed as he tossed the scraps to the floor. They were naked now and holy shit, this was really happening. Lila looked her fill of Matt and the impressive erection he was sporting, not minding one little bit that he was giving her the same lingering appraisal. His gaze strayed to her thighs and the liquid folds that beckoned between her legs.

She knew the moment he spotted her tattoo—the delicate line of ink in the shape of a heart. She also saw the moment of recognition when he realised which story she had told about her special little tatt. And what his starring role had been in that tale.

'The Tattooed Heart,' he murmured appreciatively, brushing his fingers over the curls of ink on her hip. Lila writhed reflexively. She was so wound up, it wouldn't take much effort on either of their parts for her to fulfil her end of Matt's promise. His head ducked towards her hip and Lila gasping when that clever tongue of his circled and swirled over the lines of ink there. It was close, but infuriatingly not close enough to what she wanted. She was ready to tug him closer with her fist in his hair. His hand was, even now, brushing against the soft curls at the apex of her thighs. Again, close, but *not enough*. She seized his hand instead.

'If you don't fuck me in the next thirty seconds, I may never forgive you.'

There was enough light in her tone to let him in on the joke—but enough of a snarl to also let him know she was serious. His long, slow, and thoroughly wicked smile died abruptly when he groaned, 'Condom!'

Lila wrapped her legs around his to prevent him from leaving. There was enough white knight left in Matt, even at this late stage, for him to be the responsible gentleman.

'My handbag.' She nodded just over her shoulder at her bag sitting on the bench just out of her reach. 'Inside pocket. *Now*, Matt.'

He chuckled darkly, stretched over, pushing her in the process until she was flat on her back spread out on the counter like a feast. Matt stretched himself over her, reaching into her bag and fishing out the precious rubber. His teeth tore open the packet and he fumbled the condom on his straining cock. He let out a careful breath when the latex rolled all the way down to the root. He gripped her hip with one hand and guided himself to her entrance with the other.

Hot and hard, the head eased past her labia and slid smoothly the rest of the way. She could feel her inner muscles squeezing around the foreign thickness of him and Matt closed his eyes with a shuddering sigh.

'Christ, you're tight. Hold on a sec,' he muttered. 'I've been waiting months for this. Let me enjoy this first one.'

Breathlessly, Lila watched as Matt pulled out slowly, so slowly. Then slid forward once again, maddeningly unhurried. Once he was seated down to the base, her muscles twitched around him and with a growl, he plunged back again. Pistoning in and out with controlled force at the most delicious angle that sparked across her clit with each drive. Mail scattered across the floor, flung there by her outstretched arm, her breasts bobbed each time Matt pushed, her legs wrapped around him, locking her ankles around his back.

'Don't stop!' she gasped out. '*Please!*' Her nails raked down his back, urging him impossibly closer, eliciting a growl from Matt.

'No chance,' he growled. The familiar full body tingles were starting; it wasn't far off now. Her toes curled as Matt laid another searing kiss on her, capturing her wail as the pulsing throb in her groin increased, every muscle tightening as her orgasm crested and broke. Her climax was so sudden and encompassing, it stole the breath from her lungs, her scream was silent. The roar of blood in Lila's ears deafened her and for a moment she thought she might black out. Matt, sweat dripping from his brow, gritted his teeth as he reached his own climax, hips stuttering, furiously jerking, a hoarse cry tearing from his throat.

He sagged, slumping against her, and Lila cradled him in her thighs. She feathered light caresses down his spine soothingly, his jagged breaths easing just as her heart rate slowed. Lila sighed languorously.

'I don't think we've pissed the neighbours off yet. Wanna go again?'

'Christ woman, give a man a chance to take a breath!'

Robot Dreaming
By
Kerrie Starbuck

'So, how was it?'

Hanna took a moment to enjoy the flashback that sprang to life and spreadeagled its way across her mind. A pair of hot hands on her thighs lifting her up until her legs wrapped around a waist as thick as a tree trunk, soft wet lips covering hers, devouring her, thrilling her...

Her cheeks flamed. 'Okay, I guess.'

'Okay? Just *okay*?' Her sister, Laurel, gasped her displeasure down the phone line. Hanna knew she would be frowning over the top of her tea cup. 'You haven't had a holiday in years. I finally convince you to go away for some well-earned debauchery, and that's it? Those are all the details I get? What would our dear mother say?'

Hanna rolled her eyes. 'Well, knowing Mum, she'd probably say it serves me right because I should never have started working for a *mechanical whorehouse* to begin with. Then she'd lecture me for a while about how I'm wasting all the brains the good Lord gave me. And she'd finish by going on for some considerable time about how I've brought nothing but shame and embarrassment to our family name.'

Laurel harrumphed yet more displeasure. 'I swear, if we could just convince Her Highness to take a tour of your office, maybe she'd finally get that stick out of her bum and appreciate the brilliance of what you do. I mean, for the last five years you've given up your entire social life to build robots that are so lifelike you can't tell the difference between them and humans. If that's not irony, I don't know what is.'

Laurel continued listing the robots' virtues as though she were reading from a sales brochure, but her voice faded into the background as another flashback took over Hanna's brain: a clear image of her hands running over the golden ridges of a perfectly sculpted back, lower and lower until they cupped two perfectly formed globes of masculine arse, their smooth skin marred only by a small—

'—tattoo. If it wasn't for that barcode on their hip, you'd never know they weren't one of us.'

Hanna jolted back to reality and took a sip of her own tea before selecting a chocolate chip cookie from a half empty packet. Crumbs scattered across her desk as she took a bite.

'Stop talking about their perfect bodies, Laurel! Anyone would think you're not already married to a super-hot guy who loves you so much he helped you move far, far away from our beloved mother.' She took another bite. 'There are other failsafes, anyway. They can't leave the hotels, for one. They shut down like a toy with a dead battery the moment they step over the threshold.'

'Hmm, pity. What I wouldn't give to have one of those in my cupboard at home for when Brad's away. Hey, what are you eating? It'd better not be a cookie. You're gonna get scurvy, Hanns. When was the last time you had a proper meal? Something with vegetables in it.'

Hanna crossed her fingers. 'Saturday? Um yeah, definitely Saturday.' It was pointless to argue with her sister about her diet. Their mother had gifted every one of her tall, elegant genes to Laurel. Not a single one left by the time Hanna had come along. Or so she said. Hanna sometimes thought she'd withheld them through sheer spiteful force of will. Science be damned. Regardless, she'd long ago given up trying to emulate her sister's long blonde hair and wispy figure.

She glanced down at the curvy body she'd dressed in the first clothes she'd laid her hands on that morning. The high heels had been a gift from Laurel. A touch of style she'd never have had the skill to select for herself. In fact, if she hadn't done the blood tests herself she might not have believed they were even related.

Laurel, the beautiful one.

Hanna, the smart one.

She swallowed and gathered her notepad. 'Anyway sweetie, I have to go to a meeting. Thank you again for the making me take a holiday, it was...' *Wonderful. Life-changing. Erotic as hell.* 'Great. I'll fill you in on all the details later.'

She crossed her fingers as she lied. Those R-rated memories were for her memory alone. She would hoard them for the lonely nights ahead.

Her sister chuckled, low and dirty. 'You'd better! Toodles.'

Hanna tucked her phone into her pocket and hurried through the subterranean corridors of Jenson Technology to the cavernous glass-walled boardroom. She spied the last spare chair at the back of the room and slipped into it as surreptitiously as she could. The room was already packed with sharp-eyed employees, waiting patiently for the next words of wisdom from their illustrious leader. She wasn't even sure how many people worked there anymore; there seemed to be more every week.

She bowed her head as Mr Jenson began to speak. He was not known for his good humour, only his pathological genius in the field of artificial intelligence. Her tardiness would not go unnoticed. He cast her a withering look before continuing in his usual monotonous drone. She'd learnt to switch off during his weekly team meetings, often she used the time to sketch new ideas in her notepad. Today her hands sat idle as her brain wandered to more pleasant memories—one in particular of a pink tongue leaving a cool path down her stomach, warm caramel hands encouraging her to arch her back so it could stretch her open and find its goal, swirling, licking, until the sound of her triumphant screams echoed off the ceiling...

A subtle cough from somewhere on her right dragged her mind back into the room and her cheeks flooded with colour, as though her smutty thoughts had been on display in front of the whole room instead of Jensen's latest budget projections. She glanced toward the sound and noticed a pair of caramel hands resting on a pair of hard thighs.

Not just any hands. She knew those hands.

Intimately.

She knew them because she'd just been daydreaming of those hands and the hours she'd spent on the weekend studying them as thoroughly as they had studied her.

She knew them because they were made with the synthetic skin she'd help create. The same skin that covered every one of the 'bots in the flagship Jensen Technology Hotel where she'd just spent the best two days of her life.

Her eyes followed the tanned forearms up across the broad expanse of chest and higher to his face. Twin hazel eyes stared back above a mouth that could only be described as porn-star plush. She jerked backwards as his face creased into a smile.

Impossible!

Adrenalin spiked. What was a pleasure 'bot doing in the boardroom? Was this some kind of hallucination caused by low blood sugar? Maybe she needed another cookie.

She shot up from her chair, earning a sharp look from Mr Jenson. 'I'm sorry, I'm not... feeling very well,' she murmured. 'I... excuse me.' She whirled and exited, heading straight back to the sanctuary of her office, her feet flying back down the hallways until, hyperventilating, she slammed the door behind her and leant back against it. She swiped her sweaty palms down her legs. She had to call security, she had to...

The door vibrated behind her as someone knocked. Someone big. She didn't have to be a professor of neuroscience to know who. Her hands were shaking as much as the door.

'Hanna?' A disembodied voice wove its way through the wood. 'Open up. Please?'

She knew that voice too. Only, the last time she'd heard him use those words, he'd meant for her to open her *legs* to him not her door. And god help her, she had. Wider and wider until he'd buried himself balls deep inside her, until his hips had ground against hers, again and again, culminating in the best orgasm she'd ever had.

But that had all been inside the safety of the best robot brothel in Australia. A brilliant suggestion from her loving but interfering sister who'd somehow convinced her to finally try the merchandise she'd spent the last five years of her life developing. Merchandise that had no business whatsoever being outside the hotel and inside her office.

This had to be a daydream. She must have fallen asleep in Jensen's meeting. That was the only explanation.

'Hanna,' the voice tried again. 'Let me explain.'

She clapped her hand over her mouth as a hysterical giggle escaped. Explain? Explain how a robot had escaped the hotel? Jensen was going to kill her. Or worse. Fire her. What if something had gone wrong with the coding? What if the 'bots had found a loophole? What if they were all roaming the streets? Their hotel would be out of business within a week. She'd never get another job. Her mother would be thrilled.

Damn it!

Unless she found the glitch and fixed it. If she did, then Jensen might be so grateful he'd give her that extra funding she'd been asking for...

She took a deep breath and opened the door, waving him inside. 'Come in, quickly, before someone sees you,' she hissed.

The man mountain in front of her shook his head and grinned. 'I'm kind of hard to miss, honey.' He was right. He filled her doorway like a life-size John Cena doll. Every woman's lumbersexual fantasy come to life, from the lush brown beard decorating his face, all the way down to the heavy boots planted on her floor as if they had no place better to be.

'Most people can't help but see me.' He gripped the doorframe and titled his head to one side, then sighed. 'Everyone except you, that is.'

Oh she saw him alright, she just wasn't sure how this was happening. Maybe she was hallucinating. Maybe all those glorious orgasms had knocked something loose in her brain. Maybe she wasn't the smart one anymore. It was hard to think with him looking at her with that teasing twinkle in his eyes.

She stepped back so he could enter, and so she could get away from the overwhelming man-smell of him. Something woodsy and warm. She'd have to thank the Styling department for inventing it, whatever it was. Amazing. Addictive.

He shut the door behind him and folded his arms across the chest she had roamed with impunity all weekend. She tucked her hands behind her back to keep them to herself. It wasn't enough. His body sang to her. There was something intensely erotic about knowing what was hidden under his boring suit and tie. Her office wasn't large and with him there it suddenly felt even smaller. Tiny. She scurried to put the distance of her desk between them.

When she turned back he puffed out a breath that blew out his cheeks, and pinned her with a look that could have melted steel.

'I know you're probably wondering what the hell is going on... I wish I could... maybe I should start from the beginning.' He stared at the blank ceiling as if for inspiration. 'Six months I've worked here, Hanna. Six months of flirting with you via email. Six months of enduring those tedious team meetings just to see you, just on the off chance that one day you'd look up and see me. Six months of hanging out in the lunchroom hoping to run into you and start a conversation in person. But...' He flung out his arms. 'You were always too busy working on your 'bots. I was jealous of them, I guess. That's not an excuse, I just—'

Her eyes widened. 'I'm sorry, I don't even—wait, wait. You're... Freddy? From the Finance team? But when we met, I mean last weekend, when we...' She blushed. 'You said your name was Erick.'

He sighed. 'My full name is Frederick. I didn't always look—' He gestured to his solid physique. '—like this. In high school everyone called me Fat Freddy. I know, kids are cruel, right? And ever since I became an accountant, I've been Freddy from Finance. Super original. Apparently people really like alliteration. But my mum has always called me Erick, so—'

'So you tricked me into thinking you were someone else?' Her eyes narrowed. 'Some*thing* else.'

'No, I mean, yes, I... ' He scraped his hands over his closely cropped hair and tugged his beard twice, hard. 'Look, I was over at the hotel doing my monthly audit, and who do I see standing at the reception desk, but you. Honey, you looked like some kind of Hollywood starlet in that red dress. Seriously, you stopped me right in my tracks. I'd never seen you in a dress, I thought maybe you'd come to look the place over, do your own audit. But then I realised you were checking in, waiting for them to allocate you a 'bot. And then, right at that moment, you looked up and saw me. Really saw me. My feet froze to the ground, couldn't have moved if my life depended on it, and you asked me, *Are you mine?*'

He put his hands together like he was praying. 'Jesus H Christ, I'm telling you there is not a man alive who could have looked into those gorgeous green eyes of yours and said no.'

She raised a single eyebrow over one of those said gorgeous green eyes.

He shook his head. 'You... you sounded so hopeful, so sweet, so much like every one of my fantasies wrapped up in a great big red Christmas bow. Like I said, I'm an accountant, I analyse risks for a living but right then all I could think was that this was my once in a lifetime chance. With you. So I nodded my big stupid head and the next thing I knew you were leading me off to your room and then... one thing led to another and...' He trailed off, gripping the back of his neck and staring at the floor. 'I'm sorry, Hanna.'

Her brain whirred, trying to keep up, wondering where to start unpacking all that.

This guy was the same guy she'd been chatting to at work online all day for months? The one she'd commiserated with about budget cuts, discussed every movie she'd ever seen, and shared her favourite sandwich recipes with?

And he liked her? Like, really liked her? Her and not her blonde bombshell sister?

She touched the messy brown bun she'd pulled her hair into that morning and wished she'd spent a little more time on it. Maybe put on a dress...

'So, you're not a...'

'Bot?' His mouth twisted into a grin. 'No.'

'But what about the...' She gestured toward his middle section.

'Barcode tattoo on my hip? I drew it on with a felt tip pen while you were sleeping. Don't look at me like that, I know it was insane, I was insane, it was ten kinds of fucked up. Plus it kept washing off in the shower. Don't laugh, it wasn't funny!' His grin widened for a moment, then his face turned serious. 'Hanna... please... if you don't believe anything else, believe me when I say it was the best weekend of my life.'

He folded his arms and lifted his chin, once again more monolith than man. 'But I had no right to trick you like that. So if you say the word, I'll leave this room right now and you'll never have to look at me again.'

Hanna snorted. It seemed unbelievable that a word from her could move him when the likelihood of her physically shifting him were beyond even her capability to measure. Besides, her brain had overloaded. It had given up all rational thought. In fact, she was pretty sure it was still in the boardroom somewhere. All it had left behind were some disturbingly vivid memories of the many ways this man had succeeded in pleasuring her beyond her wildest dreams.

She stared at his chest, the one she'd worshipped for hours. 'What about the receptionist at the hotel, why didn't she say anything?'

He shrugged. 'She's new. I guess she wasn't hired for her intellect.'

'But I...' *I let you lick my entire body. I shared my secret fantasies with you and we tried them all. I let down my guard and you made me feel safe. And sexy as hell. I don't think I can give that up yet. I don't think I can give you up...*

She forced herself to meet his steady hazel gaze. 'I think... I think if you're about to walk out of my life forever, the least you could do is kiss me goodbye.'

Silence pulsed around the room for a beat, then two, before his hands dropped to his hips and a smile tugged at the corners of his mouth. 'You know, that's a very good point, honey. Smart girl.'

She watched him cross the room, her heart almost pounding out of her chest as he strode around the desk and wrapped one of his giant hands around her waist, the other behind her neck. Her mouth dropped open as his fingers massaged her nape and tilted her head way, way up to look at him.

With no visible effort, he lifted her onto the desk, her bottom hitting the table with a thud. His thumb grazed her bottom lip for a moment, tugging it open further before he captured her mouth with his. Her legs fell open and invited him to settle closer between her thighs. God, she was such a slave to this man, all he had to do was touch her. His lips continued to caress hers as his growing erection brushed against her core. She groaned her approval.

His hands stroked down her back and pulled her knees up to his waist, then slid her skirt up until it was ruched at the top of her thighs. He groaned his own approval. Every inch of her skin sizzled, instantly aflame, his fingers igniting a burning trail of lust that had simmered under the surface ever since she'd walked out of the hotel.

She yanked on his tie, pulling him even closer so her mouth could re-explore the familiar contours of his. Inviting his tongue to do the same. Who would have imagined an accountant could kiss like a mechanical whore? She shoved her hands under his jacket as he pushed her body further onto the table.

Her open cookie packet flew off the edge, scattering biscuits over the floor, distracting her. Gods alive, what were they doing? In the middle of the office? What if someone caught them?

She broke off the kiss, panting as his fingers began to push aside her panties and her last shred of sanity. 'Erick—'

His face had taken on the glazed look she loved, but his eyes were focused as he traced his thumb over her cheekbone. 'I locked the door behind me. The team meeting will go for at least another thirty minutes. Trust me, Hanna, let me take care of you. Always.'

She hid a smile and slid her hand down his chest with excruciating slowness until it dipped into his pants. 'Cocky.'

He wiggled his eyebrows at her as the cock in question swelled in her palm. 'I am now.'

She ran her hand over its length, then curled her fingers around it and squeezed. He closed his eyes and moaned, pausing in his thorough exploration of her cleavage. Her other hand took care of his zipper, and pushed his dark suit pants down as far as she could. His manhood sprang free, bracketed by his smooth hipbones. She ran her hands over his skin, revelling in the way it shuddered under her touch, as though he were just as affected as she was. She gripped his arse to bring him closer still.

A random thought popped into her head and she couldn't resist peering around him at his hip.

'Are you... are you checking for a tattoo?' He rolled his eyes and performed a clumsy turn, hindered by the pants still bunched around his knees. 'Happy now?'

She giggled, an unfamiliar, carefree sound, and pulled him back to her, fitting their bodies together in a tender embrace.

All clear.

All man.

All hers.

His head dipped to plant a row of butterfly kisses along one side of her neck.

'Now Hanna honey, lean back and let me show you some things a robot lover could never do.'

And because she had always been the smart one, she let him.

Forget-Me-Not
By
Kristine Charles

She'd been thinking about it for a while now. Contemplating the prick of the needle. Hearing the hum of the machine. Thinking about the design she'd found. She could see the pattern already, a vivid stain on her pale skin, extending from the dip of her waist, ending just where hip became thigh.

She remembered suggesting that she get a tattoo one Sunday morning while they'd lazed in bed. They'd been naked, her long dark hair in a tangle beneath her head. He'd been sweeping his big hands over her pale skin. The rough skin of his fingertips followed the hollows and plains of her generous, unpainted curves. He'd glanced up at her, his blue eyes alight with mirth, and told her she was too proper for ink—even though he was covered in it.

He'd said he didn't think she'd go through with it, even as his body had moved over hers. The ink on his biceps had flexed as his arms had taken his weight, the art on his chest had rippled as he'd eased his way inside.

She'd been miffed, but easily distracted as he'd pushed into her. Any thoughts of painting her skin had been washed away by the brush of his hands, the sweep of his lips and the thrust of his cock.

And then, everything had changed.

~ * ~

Fucking hell it's cold. Abigail stood on the dark street corner. It was nine on a Friday night and their website said they'd be open, but the door was securely locked and there was no light in the dilapidated store. She glanced up and down the deserted street again, pulling her coat tighter and stamping her feet to ward off the chill. There was no-one around.

Abigail had spent the last three hours sitting at a dodgy dive bar around the corner from Viper Ink, nursing a glass of house red and waiting. She'd not been able to bring herself to drink more than three sips of the wine. She'd been told that they wouldn't tattoo her if she was under the influence and, while she wasn't usually a light-weight, she had one shot at this. If she didn't go through with it tonight, she wouldn't come back. And, for reasons she couldn't even explain to herself, she knew she had to go through with it.

She pulled the tattered piece of paper from her pocket, unfolded it with cold fingers, and looked at it again. She'd found it six months ago. Six months to the day after they'd put Aiden in the ground. It had been shoved into a drawer filled with his old papers, a drawer she'd finally convinced herself to clean out. The minute she'd seen it, she'd known. She'd loved the bright blue of the flowers and the vivid green of the leaves, the clear lines of the design and the detail of his sharp angular signature running dark alongside the curve of a leaf. It was almost as if he'd left it for her.

'Hey, sorry,' the deep voice sounded behind her as the hinges on the security door squealed in protest at being opened. 'Bit late tonight. You here for a tat?'

Abigail turned and her dark eyes widened at the burly, bearded man in leather unlocking the door. Stereotypical tattoo artist. 'Uh, yeah. I am.' She shrugged a little and stepped forward before pulling herself up, hesitating. 'I mean, I am if you can fit me in.'

'Sure. I think I've got some time. I'm Bruce.' He pushed open the door and stepped back, waving her through. 'Come on in.'

She followed Bruce inside and looked around. The interior of the shop looked nothing like she'd anticipated based on the chipped concrete, barred windows and faded paint of the exterior. It was clean, industrial. Lots of black and white and chrome and leather. And there were hundreds of tattoo designs hanging on the walls. Black and white and bright colours and watercolours. She turned around, taking it all in as Bruce bustled around the shop logging onto a sleek looking MacBook and setting up.

'So, did you have something in mind?' he asked.

Abigail nodded. 'Yes, I ...' she trailed off, moving towards him and spreading the paper on the counter. Her hands trembled as she smoothed the sheet. 'This.'

He looked down at the tattered page and nodded. 'Forget-me-nots. Good choice. That's great art and it'll suit you. Where're you looking to put it?'

'Here,' Abigail said, flattening her hand over her left hip bone. She could feel the tremor in her hand. 'Wrapped around from my waist to the top of my thigh.'

He nodded again. 'Great. Let's get the paperwork done and get started.'

~ * ~

Two hours later, it was done.

Abigail stepped outside the store and her hand fluttered beneath her coat towards the tender patch on her hip. Her fingers skimmed lightly over the dressings and her skin hummed, the slight aggravation of the irritated flesh making everything more real. She walked down the street feeling... different. Her heart ached and the threat of tears burned in the back of her throat. But she also felt lighter somehow, like she'd been holding onto a great big balloon that she'd finally let go, let float away. It was hard to articulate, even to herself. It felt like a goodbye.

Passing the bar she'd been in earlier, Abigail decided that another drink was in order. She didn't want to go home yet. Didn't want to be alone in the flat they'd shared. Wasn't ready to lie down again in the bed that had been theirs. Right now, she wasn't sure she'd be ready to do that ever again. Even the thought of being there made her queasy. She wondered if it was time to find a new place or, at least, to go shopping. She should probably buy a new bed. At least get a new mattress. When her thoughts made the queasy feeling grow, she put it all from her mind and went inside, slipping onto a stool at the battered black laminate bar and ordering a single malt scotch. Double. Neat.

Thank God for grungy back street Sydney bars that stock top shelf liquor. Abigail watched the bartender lift the dark green bottle, pour her drink and slide it towards her. He followed up with a small bowl of peanuts, took the credit card she handed to him, and went about his business as she inhaled the campfire smell of the alcohol.

'That's good whisky.'

Abigail turned her head slowly, her mind taking a few moments to process the identity of the man now standing beside her.

'Holy shit,' she breathed. 'Levi.'

He nodded, a smile softening his chiselled face as he slipped onto a barstool. 'Yeah. Hey, Abigail.'

~ * ~

Abigail hadn't seen Levi since that dark night in the hospital when Aidan had... she shook her head slightly. *Not going back there. Not now.*

He looked good, she thought. His hair was a little longer, but still dark and brushed back from his forehead, emphasising his clear green eyes. He'd grown some scruff, a dark shadow of hair extending along his jawline and around his mouth that made him seem edgier somehow. Levi had never been the edgy one. That had always been Aidan.

'Where have you been?' she asked. Her tone was measured but her fingers clenched tightly around her glass.

'Around.' He shrugged and ordered a beer. 'Spent some time in Vietnam, Cambodia, Laos. Was in Malaysia for a while. Indonesia.'

Abigail's eyebrows raised in surprise. 'You really have been around.'

'Yeah, well,' he hesitated, clearing his throat. 'I couldn't stay. Not... after.'

She nodded slowly. He and Aidan had been almost inseparable. They *had* been inseparable until she'd come along. But even then, Levi had still been around. Abigail took a long sip of her scotch and felt it warm her limbs. 'We missed you at the funeral,' she said, knowing she meant to wound him but wincing as pain shadowed his face.

'I...' He turned to the beer that the bartender had provided and drank. He glanced back at her before turning away again to drink again. 'I couldn't.'

Yeah, I didn't want to stay either but it had been necessary. The taste of bile momentarily coated her throat. She picked up her glass, took the last sip of the dark gold liquid to chase away the taste of bitterness and signalled the bartender for another. Then she looked up at Levi, saw the guilt, misery and regret in his eyes, and swallowed hard.

'So, what have you been up to?' he asked, lifting his beer to his mouth. 'Are you living around here?'

'No,' Abigail began, wondering where to start. He'd been gone for twelve months. So much had happened. So much water had passed under the bridge. 'I'm not living around here, I'm still at the flat,' she said, glancing sideways towards him and then immediately dropping her eyes to the top of the bar. 'Still working in the city.'

'At the same place?'

She shook her head. 'No, I'm at a different place now, an advertising firm. Been there about nine months.'

Levi nodded, turned back to his beer.

Well, this is awkward. She took another sip of the heavy scotch the bartender had placed in front of her. The two of them sat facing the wall of wine and liquor bottles behind the bar, side by side but a million miles apart. She could see his face reflected in the mirrors behind the bottles, his eyes focused on his beer bottle like it held the answers to the mystery of life. She could feel the words on her tongue. Those words that would make it easy for him, let him off the hook for leaving. They'd all coped in their own way. And now, as she felt the throb of the tattoo on her hip, she wanted to give him a break. But, before she could, he spoke again.

'I've been back for a while now,' he began, his eyes still on his beer. 'I've been meaning to get in touch. I tried to call a couple of times but some guy answered and...' He shrugged.

And what? 'I got a new number.'

He glanced at her. 'Oh. Right.'

'Work phone,' she continued, lifting her glass and swirling the scotch around and around. Suddenly, she brought the glass to her lips and downed it, letting out a long breath of relief even as the alcohol burned her throat. Then she signalled the bartender for a third before she turned to him. 'What were you going to say?'

He looked at her puzzled.

'When you called? What did you want? What were you going to say?'

He didn't respond for a long time. One breath. Two. She sipped at her drink and idly wondered if she'd pay for her excess tomorrow. Five breaths. Six. She could feel her heart pounding in her chest as she stared at her scotch, waiting for him to speak. Her fingertips trailed along her thigh, up towards her bandaged hip, which was starting to smart.

After twelve breaths he reached out, two of his fingers pressing on the side of her chin, turning her towards him. Then his lips were against hers. Hot and soft and demanding. And, as she shifted on the bar stool, wanting to be closer to him, some part of her brain was challenging her, questioning her judgment.

What the fuck was she doing? What the fuck was he doing? He'd been Aidan's best friend. You can't do this. You have to stop this.

She felt the pull of the bandages on her skin as she twisted awkwardly. Felt the sting of the tattooed flesh beneath and the prickle of the alcohol seeping into her brain. His warm hands cupped her face, held her still as he took her lips.

It had been so long since she'd been held, had been kissed, had been wanted. She wasn't the same person as she'd been before Aidan and, clearly, life was short. She didn't want to stop. So why should she have to?

Truth was, she didn't have to stop.

So she let him kiss her.

And she kissed him back.

~ * ~

Stumbling out of the bar, Abigail could feel Levi's fingers digging in to her ribs, first steadying her, then pushing her up against the brick wall, his warm lips still covering hers. Her heart thudded in her ears and her chest felt tight—like she couldn't get enough air—but she couldn't bring herself to care. Levi demanded all her attention. And thankfully, he was holding her up because she wasn't sure how long her quivering legs would carry her.

'My apartment,' he mumbled, the sound of his voice muffled between her breasts. 'It's around the corner...' He left the rest of his question hanging as he concentrated on pushing her coat aside and tugging her top down, flicking his tongue out to taste her skin where it pressed over the cup of her bra.

'Um,' she said, her hands wrapping around his biceps and digging in, feeling the leather of his jacket give beneath her grip. She found it hard to form words, partly because of the alcohol but mostly because his mouth was sucking a path from one side of her chest to the other and it seemed to be interrupting the neural pathways to her brain. And then there was the simple fact that this was Aidan's best friend. It seemed wrong to be contemplating... she let her thought trail off as he sucked the swell of her breast into his mouth, pulling hard enough to leave a mark. She moaned.

Levi glanced up, catching her eyes with his. 'Do you want... shit.' He started to pull away.

'No.' She slid her hands up, around his neck and into his hair, tugging him back down. 'No. I...' *What did she want?* It was clear where this could lead and she'd not been with anyone like this since Aidan got sick.

Fuck it. She stretched up, her lips meeting his. She felt his groan vibrate in his chest, his fingers clutch at her waist. He tasted of malt and hops from the beer he'd been drinking and something else, something darker and richer and... dangerous. And she wanted it. 'Your place,' she said, her lips a whisper against his.

He nodded. Swallowed. Grabbed her hand to pull her along the footpath towards his home.

~ * ~

'It's not much,' he warned, shepherding her through the doorway, his front close to her back, his hand splayed over her belly. She heard the door slam behind them and whimpered a little as his hand slipped up, beneath her coat, cupping her breast. It was hot, the heat of his skin bleeding through the cotton of her top and there was an urgent buzzing sensation starting to itch at the base of her neck.

'Jesus,' he said, shifting her coat aside and biting down on her shoulder. 'You're so soft.'

She shuddered hard at the feeling of his teeth against her skin. He turned her to the right and kept moving forward, his lips and tongue and teeth moving over her skin. Her vision caught sight of half-unpacked boxes, two bean bags and a massive television. A little further on there seemed to be a kitchen to the left and a dining area to the right. He eased her through another doorway into his bedroom. More boxes surrounded a huge bed, which appeared to have been hurriedly made with dark blue sheets and the bare minimum of pillows.

Just inside the bedroom door he tugged her around to face him, his hands pushing into her long dark hair and holding her face steady as he kissed her again. His lips slanted across hers, tongue teasing them apart, allowing him entrance. She gasped and he took the kiss deeper, backing her up until her thighs hit the mattress. Then she reached behind her, tugging her coat from her shoulders and dropping it to the floor. He followed it with her shirt, pulling it up and over her head before throwing it aside. It wasn't until he got to her skirt that he noticed the dressings on her hip.

'What the…' He pulled back, his fingers drifting across the gauze.

'Uh,' she muttered, her hands fluttering towards her hip. 'I… it's a tattoo.'

His eyes met hers and she saw the surprise. 'You got a tattoo?'

She frowned and narrowed her eyes. 'Yes. Yes. I got a tattoo. Is that a problem for you?'

'Easy there, tiger,' he said, his hands cupping her shoulders and sliding slowly down her arms. 'It's not a problem. It's just a surprise. I didn't expect…' he paused, seeing the ire rising in her eyes. 'Can I see?'

Bruce had said she could take the dressings off after a few hours but she was a bit unsure. It was her first tattoo after all. In lieu of a decision, she shrugged noncommittally.

'You got it tonight?'

'Yeah.'

She could see him thinking. 'A couple of hours then. It'll be okay to take the dressings off, and I can redress it for you.'

'How do you know about tattoos?' she asked, looking up at him a little sceptically.

He grinned and undid a few of his shirt buttons before reaching behind his neck and pulling it off over his head. The air whistled softly between her teeth as she inhaled in surprise. His arm was covered in ink, starting over his left chest and extending up over his shoulder and down his arm to his mid-forearm. She lifted her hand, fingertips gently tracing the swirls of ink from his bicep up to his shoulder and down. It was just a sort of tribal pattern for the most part until it reached his heart. There, a pocket watch had been worked into the tattoo, the chain trailing back up into the swirls of the design. The time on the watch was eleven thirty-two.

'That's the time,' she whispered, lifting her eyes to his. 'The time that Aidan ...'

He nodded.

Well, shit. She let her fingers continue to trace over the lines of the tattoo. As she traced the art she became aware of the flesh beneath. She could feel the taut muscles beneath his skin, see the defined 'v' of the muscles at his hips disappearing beneath his pants. As she watched he moved his hand to his pants, unbuttoning and unzipping, letting them hang on his hips while he took care of her skirt. He unzipped it, let it drop in a puddle of fabric at her feet, then pushed his own pants down, lifting his feet to kick the pants away.

She slipped her hands beneath the cotton of his boxers, let her fingers explore, learning his length, his girth. He seemed to lose interest in seeing her tattoo as she wrapped her hand around him, became far more interested in divesting her of her bra. When he had it off, she sat down on the bed and tugged his underwear down enough to let his dick spring free.

'Fuck, Abigail, I—' His voice cut off on a strangled moan as she wrapped one hand around him tightly, and began moving it quickly back and forth. She couldn't take her eyes off the dark pink skin, the head of his cock popping out between her thumb and forefinger as she pumped. Hesitantly she reached forward and, on the next stroke, poked out her tongue, licking at the head.

'Motherfucker,' he moaned, his fingers pushing into the hair at the side of her head, gathering a fistful of the long dark strands in his hand.

He clearly liked it. So, she did it again, and again, tasting him as he slid easily against her palm, eventually wrapping her lips around the head of his cock and sucking. He responded with gibberish, his words spilling over each other.

'Fuck. Yes. So fucking wet. I...'

Abigail kept one hand wrapped firmly around the root of his cock, steadying him as his hips thrust forward, wanting more of her mouth, her throat. She'd never been good at that, at taking a man into her throat and she didn't want him to choke her, to end this before it really began. But, even in his desire he was careful, never pushing forward harder than she could tolerate, just letting the head of his cock rub against her tongue. She whined when he used his grip on her hair to gently tug her mouth away and pulled her hand away with his own.

'Not the first time,' he said quietly, tucking his fingers in the side of her underwear and pulling them down. She leaned back on the bed to help him, wriggling back even as he slid the cotton and lace down, tickling the skin of her legs. 'I don't want to come in your mouth the first time.'

Dropping the panties on the floor, he ran his fingertips over the top of her foot and up along her calves, stopping to swirl around her knees before continuing the journey up her thighs and coming to rest between her legs. 'I want to be inside you.' He let his fingers slide into her folds and pressed inward. 'The first time.'

The feeling of his thick fingers inside her, the feel of them moving and shifting as she writhed was like nothing she'd ever experienced before. She lifted her knees high, spreading her legs apart to give him better access and he took advantage of the space, easing his fingers out of her and shifting onto the mattress. He grabbed a condom from the drawer beside the bed, rolled it on and moved between her legs, his forearms resting on either side of her head with his pelvis to the side so that he didn't put any pressure on her hip. He pressed his face against her neck, licked along the pulse of her throat, trailed kisses down over her collar bones and lower, over her breasts and ribs and belly before returning to her lips, claiming them fast and hard.

With desire burning deep in her gut, she pushed Levi onto his back, rose over him as she brought her fingers to his lips, stopping his words. His hands came up to rest on her thighs, slid around to her arse as she lifted herself. She reached between them for his cock and held it, shifting forward on her knees before sinking down and taking him inside her.

'Jesus,' he breathed, his voice tight and his fingers biting into the flesh of her thighs.

She hummed his name in reply and rose up, watching his face as he watched where they were joined, a look of hunger and awe in his eyes. 'Levi,' she breathed, sinking down to take him back inside her. 'Levi.'

'Abby,' he said, his voice rough.

'Yeah,' she sighed. For some reason she'd never really understood, only Levi had ever called her Abby and, until she'd heard it fall from his lips, she hadn't realised how much she'd missed hearing it. She lifted herself up again, sank down. She could feel the burn in her thighs, the give of his torso between her knees. She let her hands rest on his chest for a few strokes, then let them skim down over his stomach and felt the muscles there clench beneath her touch.

'Abby,' he said again, his hips pushing up more sharply now, his arms stretching up to bring his hands to her breasts. He squeezed, gently at first, and then harder as he felt her tighten around him, heard her moan. 'You like that?' he asked, testing, dragging his fingers over the soft flesh, pinching her tight nipples.

'Yes,' she gasped, slipping a finger between her legs and rubbing against her clit. 'Yes.' Her eyes slammed shut and she dropped her head back. Levi lifting his knees to brace her and to give him leverage as he thrust hard inside her.

'Oh.' She gasped, moving faster over him as he found that spot deep inside her. 'Don't stop. Don't fucking stop.'

'Not going to stop,' he grunted, one of his hands sliding over her sweat-slicked skin and between her legs, pushing hers out of the way and taking over, his fingers sliding over her wet flesh.

'Fuck.'

'Yeah?'

'Yeah.'

'Now.'

~ * ~

Abigail's eyes fluttered open and then quickly clenched shut. They'd forgotten to close the curtains and the east facing window filled the room with early morning sunlight. The brightness blinded eyes that hadn't gotten enough sleep and sliced into a head that pounded with the after-effects of too much scotch.

Jesus. She breathed slowly, trying to control the need to vomit. *What had they done?* She eased her eyes open again, taking in the clothes that had been flung around the room, the pillows in a pile on the floor, the lamp that had been upended at some point during the night.

She could feel Levi behind her, his steady breathing ruffling her hair and his hands pressed flat against her stomach. The tattoo had stopped stinging but she still knew it was there, the adhesive of the bandages starting to itch. With the image of the forget-me-nots in her mind she took a deep breath and let her eyes slip closed again.

~ * ~

'Hey,' Aidan said, his quiet voice hard to hear amid the beeping and whooshing of the machines.

'Hey,' she murmured, leaning towards him. 'What do you need?'

'You,' he said, his gaunt face stretching in a smile that didn't quite reach his eyes. He squeezed her hand as he struggled to breathe. 'I don't think it'll be long now.'

Abigail nodded, biting down on the inside of her mouth, holding back her tears. 'Okay.'

'I need,' he began, wincing as he shifted in the hospital bed. 'I need to you promise me something.'

'Anything.'

'I need you to promise me that you'll live,' he said, his voice serious. 'I know you. I know you'll need to take some time, work through whatever but, promise me that you'll find a way to live okay. Don't die with me.'

Even the teeth sinking into the inside of her lip couldn't stem her tears.

'Promise me,' he said again.

'Okay,' she managed, her throat thick and burning. 'Okay.'

'Good.' He nodded and used his grip on her hand to tug her forward. 'I love you. Lay with me.'

'Love you too,' she mumbled as she climbed onto the bed, stretching out along his side and resting her head on his chest. She snuggled up as close as she could get, feeling him sigh and listening until his heart stopped beating.

~ * ~

'You awake?'

'I miss him,' she murmured, her voice hoarse with unshed tears and her fingers intertwining with his.

'Yeah,' he said, smoothing a hand down over her hip. 'I know. I do too.'

'What are we doing?'

He slid his hand across her body, cupping a breast, pulling her back into the curve of his body. 'I don't know,' he began, his hand rubbing small circles against her skin. 'I was surprised when I saw you last night. You'd been on my mind a bit, which is why I'd tried to call a few times but when the guy answered...' She felt his shrug. 'Last night I was pacing around the apartment, couldn't settle, thought I'd go down to the bar for a quick drink.' He pressed his lips to her shoulder. 'And there you were. I wanted to apologise, but I couldn't find the words. Then...' He shrugged again.

Abigail nodded. 'What do you want?'

'I want...' He leaned over, rolling her onto her back, his hand flat against her bare stomach. 'I need to see you. I... this feels weird but... I want to explore something with you.' He ducked his head, pressed his lips to hers and kissed her softly. 'It's something we should explore.'

'Yes,' Abigail said, her lips moving against his. She arched up as his hand slid lower, his warm skin leaving a tingling trail in its wake. And then his fingers rubbed at the edge of the dressing.

'Hey. I never got to see the tattoo,' he said. 'What did you get?'

Abigail pushed her shoulder against his chest, encouraging him to give her room to roll onto her back. He shifted, throwing the covers back and giving her space, his eyes glowing with an appreciation of the contrast between her pale skin and the dark blue sheets. She tugged on the dressings and he moved to help, gently peeling the sticky edges away from her skin. Slowly, they revealed the spray of forget-me-nots, still a little red and angry at the edges, but clearly stunning. She lifted her head, wanting to see.

'Bruce does good work,' she breathed, her hand hovering over her hip.

'Don't touch,' Levi cautioned her quietly as he looked at the pretty tattoo. 'Forget-me-nots. It's beautiful.'

It's my closure. She nodded as he reached out his hand, let his finger brush the curve of her thigh before pulling it away.

'He'd want you to be happy.'

Abigail sat up, wrapping her arms around the back of his neck and pulling his face towards hers. 'Yes,' she said, a smile crinkling the corners of her eyes. 'I think he'd want us both to be happy.'

'Yeah,' Levi agreed, his lips forming the word against hers before he kissed her again. 'He would.'

The Nuances of Tattooed Love
By
Josephine Brierley

I sit and watch as she works on the young guy's back; his hands grip the side of the chair, knuckles white. The sound of the needle as it scratches his skin, combined with the thunderclaps outside, creates a perfectly weird night. That and my sex-crazed thoughts as I gaze at this beautiful woman executing her craft.

I'm soaked through—my jeans only just beginning to dry out now I've been out of the rain for the time it takes heavy denim to breathe again. I'd left Stephanie over an hour ago. I was wandering the streets, with no destination in mind, the rain becoming heavier. Mojo's Ink was the first door that I came across.

I wonder if the blonde is Mo or Jo?

I suppose I look like a freak. All wet and silent, staring at her. To her credit, she remains focused on the job at hand for the most part—much to my disappointment, because when she does look up, the baby blue eyes are breathtaking. Her blonde hair is in an updo; it rests messily on the top of her head. The small stud in the side of her nose glitters under the lights, as do her long, drop earrings. With little makeup, she's naturally beautiful and so different to the woman who I thought loved me. As a tattoo artist, I would have expected this woman's skin to be painted. Instead it's cream-coloured with scattered freckles on her nose. Clean, except for the two tattooed dots I see occasionally as she flicks her wrist while she works.

I lean my back against the cold window, my skin cool as I sit and ponder. I don't know what I'm feeling. Is this heartbreak? If it is, I'm doing okay. I think it's more like disenchantment about the fact that I have given four years to a woman who I thought I'd marry one day. The fact that those four years mean nothing to her. She'd found someone else. I could handle that. People change; their wants and needs become something that only certain people could provide. She'd wanted a baby.

I couldn't give her that.

Apparently, he can.

My eyes close as I feel the water well. Can't be looking the broken man in this tough guy place. A hulky-looking guy sits at the front counter, obsessed with whatever is on the laptop before him. He didn't quiz me when I'd entered the store, allowing me to sit peacefully. The blonde dabs gently at the guy's back. He stretches his arms while she takes a moment. She stands and walks over to me. Seeing her fully, I appreciate her body for the first time. White skinny jeans, a black tee, and strappy sandals that reveal another tattoo on the top of her foot. A lotus.

I remain still, gazing up as she stands before me. Her face empty of any emotion, for which I'm pleased. I think that maybe I just want to be anonymous tonight and not tell my story. Perhaps we could lose ourselves in each other for the night. I imagine being buried deep inside her. *That* would successfully shut down the outside world… she is sexy as…. Mentally, I slap myself. I'm getting way ahead here.

'So, do you know what design you'd like?'

Ah, she assumes I'm here for my torture, some ink of my own. I hadn't really thought about another tattoo, but now, on a whim, it could be an option.

'I have something in mind. I'll wait till you finish.'

I extend my time with her, not wanting to leave just yet. My house has only memories inside anyway and right now I don't want to face any of them. She nods, tells me she'll be another half hour and returns to the guy who's now watching us. She asks him how he's feeling, makes him drink some water, softly dabs at his back with a cloth, not revealing anything when he asks. Her voice is soft. Caring.

'I want you to see it complete. Wait until I'm done.' She throws me one more glance. Her eyes blink slowly and then she lowers her head.

Leaning back, the buzz of the needle soothes me into another lull. I wonder if I hadn't walked in on Stephanie, when, or if, she would have told me. They'd been sitting on the patio, drinking wine—not in bed—but I knew. The guilt had given them away. I'd suspected it for a while now. Her boss. *So clichéd.*

In hindsight, it was all so obvious. Late nights, overnight conferences, hushed phone calls. The black lacy underwear that I'd never seen until discovered in the wash basket. She'd denied the accusations, our fights became more frequent, our sex life less frequent. We'd become roommates sharing a bed. I was the proverbial doormat. Like she'd washed the mud off onto me, cleansed herself and moved on. *I need to do the same.*

I wake to my shoulder being prodded. Sitting beside me, the tattoo artist wears a smile that melts me, her eyes full of concern. We're alone now. Hulk has left, as has the skinny kid. It's just me, her and a Luke Bryan song in the background: 'Crash my Party.'

'So, what will it be?'

You. Naked. Lying before me, exposed.

I envisage her bare, pale skin, my tongue licking her nipples that would react to my touch. I imagine what sounds she'd make when I thrust inside her, made her come.

'How are you at covering something?'

She beams, a lopsided cheeky grin. 'That depends. Are we talking a tattoo here, or a crime?'

I like her wit. She makes me forget the reason I walked in the rain to get here tonight.

'A tattoo. A name.' She nods, sincerely. She's seen it all before, I'm sure. Stupid men who permanently etch a woman onto their skin, a lifetime memory that ends up being the worst mistake of their life.

'Show me what you've got.'

She turns her head to the side, querying me. Challenging me perhaps. The way she watches me, she looks so damn cute.

I stand, grip the still damp shirt at the nape of my neck, and pull it off one handed. Her eyes narrow a little, her discreet swallow enough to tell me I've impressed her. Her finger reaches out, trailing my skin from my shoulder to my abs. I try not to be affected. *It's bloody hard though.* A line of fire burns me. She follows the swirls of ink, tracing the name inside the heart. *Stephanie.* It's small script, surely it could be erased. At the very least, masked by ink. Eventually my mind—my heart—will recover, I'm sure. Her hand stops at the waist of my jeans, her finger lingering inside, the fire still burning.

'I think a bird. I would've suggested an eagle...' Her eyes raise from my chest as she drops her hand, my own eyes lock with hers. 'If I had more space, the eagle would be perfect. Depicting strength, virility. With this small area though, I think a lark. The bird might be small, but it's symbolic of a new dawn, renewal and good fortune.'

Holy shit.

I can't turn away, there's a tightness in my chest. I swallow the lump that's now appeared in my throat. Those words hit the mark. Tonight I imagined the rain washing away the hurt. *I fucking need that new beginning.*

'So, a lark. Not too feminine?' I ask her.

'I don't think so.'

I nod, still taking her in. She's even more beautiful up close. Her eyes. The glisten of turquoise blue tells me she's a confident woman, one who strives for what she wants in life. The small wrinkles around them tell me she laughs. The dark shadows beneath a reflection of her own fears.

'Ok. I'm going to trust you. Let's do this.' The corners of her lips turn up and she leads me to her chair. I wait as she straddles the stool on wheels, preparing her needle and the ink.

Signalling me to move forward, I do as I'm told. She wipes the area, then the whir begins once more. I close my eyes as it pierces my skin, not because of any pain—I'm quite numb. I'm thankful—relieved that the reminder will be gone. I'll look to a mirror and see this as a symbol of strength, as this woman describes. I close my eyes because.... *Her name?*

Suddenly, I raise my hand to stop her. 'Shit. How rude am I? I'm sorry, I'm Blake.' She laughs and I shrug. 'It's been a long day.'

'That's okay; I'm sorry too. Normally I'd introduce myself.

You just didn't seem to want to talk. I'm Maya.'

Maya. Immediately I think it becomes her. The name appealing, much like her. She grins at me.

'It's nice to meet you.'

The gun twitches and she becomes engrossed in my chest again. Relaxing now, I let her finish. It's quicker than I thought and before long, the room is silent. I watch as she cleans my chest, then raises a mirror for me to inspect her handiwork. *Amazing.* The wings cover the name, the bird's in flight, the outline of the heart has disappeared. The claws look as if the bird is about to seize something, its beak closed, focused. She waits patiently as I admire it, then she covers the ink with plastic.

'Thanks. You do great work.'

'It's something I love doing.' She's blasé.

I reach for my shirt, but her hand finds mine, stopping me. I glance into her eyes, see the question, and even though there's nothing I'd like more than to lose myself within her, I get dressed. I sense her disappointment when I stand, or maybe it's embarrassment. I find my wallet and pay her instead.

'I'm sorry, Maya…' Something crosses her face that I can't read. 'I'm just not in the right frame of mind tonight.'

'It's fine. Would you like a drink? I sense that you don't want to be alone, my flat is upstairs. I promise to keep my hands to myself.'

I laugh with her. Loving that despite my brush-off, she's still a decent human. They're hard to find, you know, people who would place your feelings before their own.

Instinct tells me I shouldn't brush this moment aside. We've met for a reason.

So, this is how we end up sitting on her couch. She holds a wine, me a whisky. I'm glaring at her ceiling, wondering if it will help me to share my thoughts. Perhaps she could be the best person to divulge them to, a complete, yet somehow welcoming, stranger. She doesn't know me. She may judge, she may have opinions, but hey… after tonight, I don't have to see her ever again.

Those thoughts make me feel safe. I don't fear her betrayal, she's a stranger.

Betrayal can only be delivered by those you love, those you trust most, those who you give everything to. The knife of deceit is sharp and painful when polished with love.

Her perfume, sweet yet exotic, permeates the room. It's reminiscent of a tropical island. An escape. She's my escape. I was certainly tempted; I mean I was insane for denying her, and I can't explain why. Too soon? Would it fix anything? I'm having second thoughts.

Her flat is roomy, furnished sparsely, splashed with colour. The red cushions on the black couch, the colourful crocheted throw, three pink flamingos on the shelf. She sits beside me, her legs tantalisingly close. I long to place my palm between her thighs, to feel the heat that would certainly be radiating from her skin. It would warm my icy heart. I sense she has her own troubles. She seems nervous to have me here, in spite of her invitation.

'So, how long have you been tattooing?' I'd needed company. Happy that I chose to stay, now I want to know more about her. I push my confused thoughts to one side and launch into normal conversation.

'Just over five years. I've always loved to draw. To sketch. It led me here, to Mojo's, and Maurice took me in. First as an apprentice and now I do my own work. He's a wonderful mentor. Without him, I'd be lost.'

I laugh a sudden burst. 'So... Maurice is Mo?'

She nods in affirmation.

'A big guy like that called Maurice. It's funny that's all,' I explain as she looks confused.

'He looks all tough, tattooed all-over, but he's a softie at heart. A year ago his wife, Joanne, she left him. He stayed in town, kept the business going.' Her gaze asks me if I understand and we both laugh. 'What can I say, they liked their names.'

'That would have been tough for him.' I can't help but compare my situation with his. I suppose you do what you have to do.

'It wasn't my business really. I had my own worries, but he knew I was there for him if he needed me.'

My assumptions are correct. A small silence ensues as I give that more thought.

'What?' she says as I continue to stare at her.

'You.' She doesn't say anything to my one-word response. I mean what could she say? 'You strike me as someone who has their shit together, and right now my walls have crumbled. I'm wondering what I've to do to get back to being me. To being someone that would never brush off a beautiful woman such as you.'

Despite the compliment in that statement, she remains quiet, reflective, and appears awfully sad. Instantly, I want to take back whatever it was I said to upset her.

'I'm sorry, Maya. Are you okay?'

'Sure, sorry. I was just thinking about something.'

I knew that was a cop-out, but I let it be.

'The tattoo on your foot, the lotus. I'm guessing it has a meaning?' In response to her puzzled look, I continue, 'Earlier, you explained the bird in my tattoo so descriptively. I can only see two tattoos on you, so I'm guessing both have significance.' I love that she gave my tattoo a meaning. It shows her passion. I can't imagine that she'd permanently mark her own skin with anything that wasn't meaningful to her.

'The lotus…'

She removes her sandals and places her foot on the couch beside me, so I can see it more clearly. The watercolours are pink and blue, delicate lines of green surround it. My hand moves to her foot, tracing the outline of the flower—softly, almost tickling her. She doesn't move.

'It's a metaphor I suppose. The lotus is a plant that thrives in mud. When life gets tough, it reminds me I, too, can flower and grow. The mud reflects common ground we all share at different times in our lives. We all struggle at some point, and the lotus flower opens its petals one by one. It urges me to take everything day by day, always becoming stronger, overcoming obstacles.'

She amazes me. I'm still not sure what her hard times have been, but her inner strength resonates with me. I need to know more.

'Maya… that's beautiful. And the other?' It's as if she knew the question was coming. Her eyes water and again I feel I've gone too far. She takes a deep breath; her body shudders as she releases it.

'The semicolon tattoo. It's a tribute to my brother.' Her voice breaks, she struggles as tears wet her eyes. I rub her back in a futile effort to console her.

'I'm sorry, Maya. I didn't mean to pry.'

She shakes her head. 'No, it's okay. I want to tell you... Jason, he committed suicide just over two years ago. For the life of me I can't comprehend how someone believes that's the only solution to their problems. It's so final. So devastating for all those left behind.' She cries, then rushes to wipe the tears away with the back of her hand. 'This tattoo represents love and hope to those struggling with depression, suicide, mental illness— those who deem life hopeless. Because it's not. If you allow it, your story continues. You're the author. Your life is the book.'

Her voice is laced with heavy emotion, but her words captivate me.

My problems seem trivial in comparison. I feel like a selfish prick for even considering my own issues.

Her face is in her hands. She leans forward, composing herself. Moving closer, my arm surrounds her, drawing her body in. Cradling her to me, I have this urge to make her feel safe. I want to fight her battles for her. It's been a long time since I've been able to offer that to someone. Stephanie had been distant for some time. I'd given up after far too many rejections of intimacy. I'd put it down to her being stressed over not being able to fall pregnant, or perhaps work was busy. My head was too far up my arse to see what was actually going on right under my nose. She'd sought shelter elsewhere.

'Tell me what happened. How did you find me tonight?' she changes the subject.

How indeed? Fate has a strange way of interrupting your life with what it thinks is required.

I caress her arm in what must seem a nervous gesture. She has opened up to me, so I'm sure she expects me to do the same. I struggle to hold myself together. I had enough trouble being open in a long term relationship, let alone with someone I have only just met. Still, I tell her just the same.

'I discovered my girlfriend of four years cheating on me. I thought one day we'd be married. An affair... I'd suspected for some time, but now that I'm faced with it, well… It's a bit hard to take.' I swallow hard. 'But my story is nothing compared to yours, Maya. I feel so shallow. I'm sorry.'

'No, please don't. Your problems are just that… your problems. Each of us has their own demons to deal with.'

I sit silently, considering that. She's right, but some problems are nothing compared to others.

'It's not really a demon, Maya. It's a consequence of someone else's actions. It's feeling like you've been made a fucking fool of. How did I not see it?' I felt so stupid today, walking into my own home and finding them there together. Drinking wine. Holding hands. They were surprised for a moment, then Stephanie stood and attempted to speak to me. I didn't want a bar of it—didn't want to hear whatever lame excuse she had. So I left. 'Yet with all you've been through, you're strong. You live your life and I'm here feeling sorry for myself.'

'You think I have my shit together? Definitely not, Blake. I still cry every other night. Too many unanswered questions. I still wonder why Jason couldn't have spoken to me about his problems. I would've helped him. I loved him immensely. Instead, he ended his life. With a note that actually explained nothing. My mother and I left to do nothing but mourn him and forever feel some responsibility at not being able to save his life. It all seems so pointless.'

I hold her again, unable to comprehend the pain she must feel. The loss.

How does one move past such a traumatic experience and live their life without a person that meant so much to them? I remain silent. She seems to be speaking as the thoughts come to her. I don't want her to stop.

'Why were you walking in the rain?' she asks me.

'I walked out of the house, no car keys with me. I didn't want to go back in once I'd left; they were both still there. So, I just walked, the rain wasn't heavy at first. Once the storm started I walked through the first door I found. And there you were.'

She sits up, burying her legs beneath her, turning to face me. I want to see her face, the eyes that are so deep in colour they are impossible to escape. My hand lifts to her cheek. She leans into my touch, closing her eyes briefly and opening them to find I'm still fixated on her. The warm feeling inside my gut intensifies and I lean forward just a little more so that my lips are close to hers, her breath tickles my skin.

If I move just an inch more, our lips would touch. Since I had insinuated I wasn't interested downstairs, I'm hesitant. But the way her eyes absorb every little thing about me, the way her skin feels beneath my touch, the way she looks, it's so alluring. It feels like we're connected like we're the last two people on earth and we're destined to be.

When my lips brush hers, she doesn't shy away. I kiss the corner of her mouth, trail my lips to her eyes, kiss her lids when she closes them. Taste her salty tears. I cradle her head in my palms and kiss her cheek. Her breathing is steady, but heavy. She frames my face with her hands and she slams me with her lips, this time invading my mouth with her tongue. I meet her with the same fervour.

This is what a first kiss should be: fire in your bones, sinking but floating all at once. We taste each other and I feel alive. It changes everything. Hearing her moan, my name with such passion, I'm hard at the sound.

I pull away, yet she doesn't let me go. She continues to stare at me passionately. Her eyes glisten, her mouth slightly agape. Her breathing is heavy, her chest moving fast. I close my eyes. The pull too strong.

'I'm sorry,' she whispers to me.

She thinks I'm regretting what I've done. Instead, I'm thinking that was the best moment of my life so far. I'm honest with her.

'Are you kidding? You rocked my world, please, don't apologise. Come here.' I sit back against the couch, so that my front is to her back, and I manoeuvre her to be sitting between my legs. I want her to keep talking to me.

'Tell me about your brother. Was he older or younger?'

We chat—a comfortable discussion about me, Maya, her brother, and a little about my now ex-girlfriend. She explains more about Jason—about how close they were growing up, he only two years older. As kids, they had played together on an even keel. As teenagers, he had protected her. If any of his friends even looked at her, they soon regretted it. As adults, they grew further apart. The trials of life interfering with their relationship; he was committed to his work, his career.

'Did he have someone special in his life?'

'He didn't date often and there was really only the one girl I remember meaning anything to him. Mum and I met her. It only lasted a year. He never discussed her after that.'

I tell Maya about my job on the oil rig—how I'm away from home often, usually seven days at a time. While I love my job, it's remote and I suppose it gave Stephanie the opportunity to look elsewhere. She'd wanted a baby. Unconventionally, getting married first wasn't a prerequisite. For the last year we'd tried, albeit unsuccessfully.

'I suppose she thinks this other guy might be better at it. I don't know. It's really hard not to be cynical.' She leans into me as we speak. Our glasses are empty, but neither of us move. Remaining together becomes the priority.

'Do you think that maybe fate played a hand? I mean... a baby is for life. I don't understand her not wanting to be married, to be in a lifelong relationship with the father of her child,' she says to me without turning.

'I know. It's something I never questioned then, but now I see it as selfish. But you know, Maya, a piece of paper doesn't mean a marriage is forever.'

She sits up suddenly, with a determined look she turns to me. 'My parents would still be married if dad hadn't been killed by a drunk driver when I was younger. My mother never moved on. He was the love of her life, she says. It's not the piece of paper, it's the vows you take, the words you say, the promise you make to each other in your hearts.'

I can only shake my head and move forward to kiss her. My heart melts a little. This woman believes in love. She has morals. This afternoon my opinion of the human race had diminished, but this woman gives me faith.

'In this day and age, that's a rarity. *You're* a rarity, Maya.' My resolve snaps, I want to taste her.

Kissing her again, I push her gently back, manoeuvring so that I'm laying atop of her. I'm ablaze with sensation, as I roam the curves of her body. My lips leave imprints along her neck as she stirs below me. I know I could be rebounding here, yet something draws me to her. I want more with her, even if it's just one night. I kick my shoes off. I feel her hands beneath my shirt. My muscles throb beneath her touch, the smooth skin of her palms. I'm trying hard not to grind my hips into her, but she must feel me. My dick is hard, affected by her.

I rip my shirt over my head and my chest captivates her. She doesn't question why I've changed my mind, neither do I. Instead, I relish the moment. This gorgeous woman wants to spend time with me. When she stops me, stands and leads me to her bed, I follow. My uncertainties vanish. I'm going with the flow. Living in the moment.

She kisses me once and lays back. I kneel beside her, slowly removing her jeans. I trace her panty line with one finger; the scrap of lace isn't covering much. I trail my fingers along the softness of her belly and lift her shirt until her breasts are exposed, finding a pale blue lace bra. She arches her back when I push a cup to one side and lick her nipple. It stands to attention and I do the same to the other side. Suddenly impatient, I take hold of the soft fabric covering her pussy and pull. It tears apart without too much effort. She's exposed, her body perfect.

'Oh, fuck,' she mutters, sitting up.

I undo my belt and she lowers my zipper, then helps me remove my jeans and boxers. Kneeling before each other, she reaches behind and unclips her bra. It drops from her arms seductively. We stay still, each admiring each other. At this moment I need her, want her. I'm barely holding back, but I take it slow. I will savour this. My delay has her questioning me again.

'Second thoughts?' she asks when I don't make a move.

'Not at all.' I shake my head, offering her a smile. 'You're an exquisite woman, Maya. I thank whoever led me to you tonight.'

Once I kiss her, I can't stop. I caress every inch of her beautiful body, tantalisingly slow. Opening her legs wide to me, I flick her clit with my tongue. I fuck her hard, once from behind. It is raw, driven by the hunger we have for each other. Then I make love to her, slow and meaningful. We kiss with passion, touch with reverence. Perhaps it's too meaningful for a first time meeting, a one night stand. There's something here though and as she lay in my arms in the darkness, thoughts swirl in my head.

Why have I found her now?

Why couldn't it have been a month, or two months from now—however long I need to recover from my betrayal? She doesn't seem the type for one night stands. But even after I have explained what happened, she still wants me. I start questioning if I ever loved Stephanie, but quickly realise now is not the time to do that. Maya is a breath of fresh air. I do know I don't want to just chalk this up as a rebound fuck and be done with it. I need to chance fate, and I hope she chooses to as well.

'Maya....'

'Mmm....'

'I don't want this to end. You've been sent my way for a reason, and I think I know why, but I need slow.'

'Take your time, you need it. I'll be here.'

'Maya...'

'Yes....'

'Dinner, tomorrow night?' I laugh, it is all the time I need.

It's late, just before midnight. Yet we're making plans and I am feeling serendipitous. Finding something good without looking for it is not something to be taken for granted. People gravitate towards each other like magnets, the force fields too strong to ignore. The purpose, the motivation behind it all, is all part of the discovery. In life, we meet people for two reasons: they need you in their life to help them change it, or you need them in your life to help you change yours. It's destiny. It's kismet.

The Scorpion King
By
Wren St. Claire

Egypt 3200 BC

Hathor stood on the roof of her palace, her heart beating hard as she watched the enemy assemble on the plain below. Her palms were damp, slipping on the mace and shield she held. Sweat rolled between her breasts, underneath the leather shirt, her kilt clung damp to her legs. The sun was a great orange orb in the sky; the air was heavy with heat. They had come down the river in boats last night, hundreds of them, piling out onto the plain surrounding her home, invading her land as if it already belonged to them. *To him.*

The Scorpion King. He controlled all the land from the southern border at Abu to the Great Green Sea in the north. All the kingdoms had bowed to him, the length of the Nile. All except her small patch between upper and lower Egypt, Tarkhan, the remnants of the kingdom of the chiefs of the Eastern Desert, the Techenu. The cloying smoke from her vassal Hedjwer of Turo's defeat still hung in the air. Her tiny kingdom, just south of the great empty plain of Giza, had held out the longest, but they were surrounded now, with nowhere to go. Even if they could have fled back to the Eastern Desert, it would offer them no succour. It was the end for her people and for her.

She scanned the ranks of the enemy as they milled and settled into well-disciplined lines, archers first and, behind them, foot soldiers armed with javelins and daggers, or, like her, mace and shield. A man, taller and broader than the average, emerged from the ranks of men, his bronzed skin glistened in the sun, his kilt a distinctive red instead of white, as he raised a mace and spoke. Distance took the words on the wind, but the tenor was clear enough. His men roared their support in response. Even without the twin feathers of Kingship in his headdress, she would have known it was him. Her heart thumped and nausea roiled in her gut. *Goddess Neith if you love me, help me now!*

She descended the mud brick steps to the compound below where her band of fifty brave men awaited her orders. With a nod to her sandal bearer, Den, she raised the mace and her voice. 'For Tarkhan!'

Her men responded with a great roar 'For Tarkhan!' and she turned and led them out the gates of the royal compound onto the battle field, which was nothing more than a strip of level open land bordered by the river on her right and desert on her left. It was the end of the hot season and the land was barren, cracked and dry, waiting for the Nile to rise and bring new rich soil to its banks.

She brought her troop to a halt and stood with feet planted. She waited, her heartbeat so loud in her ears it was deafening. The heavy mace pulled at the muscles in her arm. She flexed it to relieve the tension.

Scorpion spoke with a man by his side, a sandal bearer by the look of his leopard skin. The man nodded and began the long walk towards them. Relief flooded her body. He didn't mean to slaughter them. He would offer them terms? She gulped air, swallowed the ache of unshed tears in her throat. How to avoid the complete humiliation of surrender? An idea came to her. As unpalatable and terrifying as it was, she had no choice. For her people's sake... She turned to her sandal bearer, Den. 'See what he wants. If you have the opportunity, ask parley.' Den nodded and stepped out to meet Scorpion's man.

~*~

It worked! Her plan worked. Hathor paced about her palace bedchamber, her soft white pleated gown hung transparent as gossamer from her shoulders, clasped at the waist by a carnelian and turquoise belt. Her oiled thighs rubbed together and she stopped, brought up short by the sight of the red coverlet and fresh linen sheets on the bed—her marriage bed. She had avoided both slaughter and humiliation. She had made a bargain that only a Queen *could* make.

Her heart fluttered as she turned back towards the wicker chest and poured herself a goblet of wine to try to still the surge of panic. She had made a bargain, for the sake of her people. Bound herself body and Ka to the Scorpion King. She could not balk at it now, no matter how much the thought of submitting to him both angered and terrified her. Would he be savage? Vindictive? Triumphant? Brutal?

She shivered despite the heat and gulped the wine.

'May I have one of those?'

His voice, deep and commanding, cut across her thoughts and she turned, her heart thumping wildly, her pulse racing.

He stood just inside the curtain, letting it fall behind him. His head reached above the lintel, he must have stooped to come through the door. He wore a plain white linen kilt tied at his waist, not his battlefield red. Like her, he had divested himself of his crown and weapons after the marriage ceremony. He was bare-foot and bare-chested. The tattoo of his namesake, the scorpion, proudly displayed on his left pectoral, symbol of his protector Goddess, Serqet. He came to her as a man only. Not a Horus. Not a King. Her pulse skittered. A man. And what a man. She swallowed. He dominated the room. Dominated *her*. Her spine stiffened. She ignored the sudden twitching pulse between her legs, the rush of heat that pooled low in her belly. She would not submit easily to his brutal will.

'Certainly,' she spoke with formality, her throat tight. She reached for the wine jar, watching him watching her. The tension stretched between them.

What is he thinking? Feeling? His face was difficult to read, his jaw square and firm and his expression hard, his nose prominent and his eyes deep set and hooded beneath winged brows. It was a harsh face, yet it was rumoured women swooned at the sight. It wasn't his physique or his features that made him irresistible to them. It was his power. It surrounded him like a cloak. Heka poured off him, the power of the God that resided within him called to the Goddess in her. She stiffened her legs. She would not fall at his feet.

She poured him a goblet of wine and held it out silently.

He stepped forward and took it from her. Their fingers touched and she trembled with the shock she felt all the way to her core. It was the first time they had touched; it took her breath. *Goddess help me!*

~*~

Scorpion raised the goblet and watched her over the rim.

He had heard tales of her, the fire Queen of Tarkhan. He had discounted the stories of her beauty. People always exaggerated. But he *had* believed the ones of her toughness and prowess in battle, and he'd expected a woman who looked and behaved more like a man to lie behind those stories. Tarkhan was the last piece of Egypt to go under his mace and he had been determined to have it, and thus fulfil his vision of a united Egypt. He had come expecting her defiance and equally anticipating her eventual surrender, bloody or willing, it would happen, he'd had no doubts of that.

Yet she had surprised him.

She'd led her warriors onto the field and faced him down with a mace and shield. She was too shrewd to fight him though; he'd demanded surrender, reluctant to shed any more blood. She'd asked parley and took him to a tent on neutral ground to discuss terms. Up close he found that she was short and curvaceous and young, with a mane of fiery hair and big blue eyes in a sharp boned face. And beautiful, as luminously beautiful as the moon of her namesake Goddess, Hathor, and as tough and battle hardened as the Great Warrior Goddess, Neith. A Techenu Queen, descendant of the desert Kings, her colouring was so strikingly different, it alone would have made her remarkable.

As it was, she stole his breath and his senses with one look. He wanted her, and she knew it. Wanted her as much as he wanted her land. She had read him easily enough. And bargained like an equal. There was no hint in her demeanour that he held the power seat. He admired and respected that. It was no hardship to acquiesce to her terms. Her people kept safe, and in return, she would agree to marry him. She would agree... he was amused by her condescension. He had women a plenty to fill his bed, but no Queen to rule at his side. It was a fitting time to choose one and she was a fitting candidate for the role. He made decisions quickly and this one wasn't difficult.

Now she lifted her own goblet in acknowledgement and he felt the same rush of want he felt on first seeing her. Her strength made his pulse skip, his body ached with a savage desire that set his blood pumping; it made him hard, ready to take her.

He tossed back the wine and set down the goblet beside hers. She stiffened as he moved closer and he noticed the pulse beat in her neck. Her skin was very fine; he caught a whiff of lotus and a base note that must be her own scent. He took a deeper breath, wanting more of her perfume. Her eyes widened and he wondered at the glimpse of alarm in them. *Is she afraid of this? Of me?*

He put up a hand to touch her delicate, fine-boned face. Her skin was smooth and soft; by contrast, his palm was big, callused and rough. He slid his fingers into her hair, behind her neck, his thumb rested under her jaw. Her lips, stained with berry juice to make them redder, fuller, more enticing, parted slightly on a faint hitch of breath and he sensed the pulse of her heart beneath his thumb.

To hold a woman and kiss her... He hadn't done that in a long time. Not since Ty died... since he'd lost his heart and his home. He deflected the memory. Loss and heartache had no place here and now. He'd slaked his needs in many women's bodies since then, but he'd not kissed them. Not held them as if they were precious and breakable. This one felt different. Was different. He wanted to kiss her, lose himself in her, put aside the burdens he carried alone for just a few moments of sweet release. With her surrender he had it all, the whole of Egypt under his sway. With her body beneath him, he would complete his dream.

He lowered his head and touched his mouth with hers. She pulled back a fraction and then pressed forward into his kiss with a trembling determination that spoke more of will than willingness. Her mouth sent tingling pleasure, arrowing straight to his groin, and he grew harder. She tasted of the wine, sweet and fruity. He circled her slender waist with his arm and pulled her against him, deepening the kiss, exploring her mouth. His blood surged with a heightening of that aching need he had been conscious of from the moment he saw her.

He moved his mouth over hers, seeking with lips and tongue to coax her response. She held still at first, like a trapped animal. Instinctively he shifted slightly, drew her closer, gentled her. She was a sweet elixir. Did she hold back to make him burn? If so, it worked. Fire Queen indeed. Her Heka ignited a flame of need that made his blood race, his breath come short and his body ache. She was Egypt. She was his.

~*~

Intoxicating. His kisses were more powerful than the wine and a complete surprise. She had expected brutishness, not tenderness. She had expected him to demand her submission, not her participation. His lips and tongue made her knees weak, made her pulse race, made her pant with sudden burning heat.

Her arms wrapped around his neck, one brushing against that tattooed scorpion, but she didn't feel its sting, barely noticed that she was touching it, because his mouth distracted her with pleasurable sensations that made her melt. When he pulled her against his body and she could feel the heat and firmness beneath his kilt, moisture between her legs bloomed and her flesh twitched and pulsed with a sharp aching need. Her knees buckled and she clung to him. *Sweet Goddess!* She panted. She moaned.

He lifted his head a fraction to appraise her; his eyes were liquid mirrors of her own desire. He surprised her yet again by letting her go and seizing the wine jar to pour them more wine. She reached for the table to prop up her weakened legs and strived to appear more composed than she felt.

'Come sit with me a moment,' he motioned her to the bed. She came with her wine goblet clutched like a weapon of defence. She sat gingerly beside him, a space of two palms between them. He leaned back, lounging on one arm, and she was forced to slew around to face him. His gaze ran over her body, the thin fabric of her loose gown hid little.

Why did he stop kissing me? Did I do something wrong? Her normal confidence had deserted her in this new game of seduction. She was out of her depth and sure that it showed. *What is he thinking?*

'When did you last lie with a man?'

His question took her breath. 'What?' She managed after a moment's struggle.

He frowned at her and the harshness she had noted earlier came back. 'It's a simple question. I should have asked it earlier, but I hadn't had leisure to think things through.'

'What things?'

'I want to be sure any child you bear is mine,' he spoke somewhat sharply, as if she was suddenly dim witted. It was an abrupt change from the consideration he had just shown her. She was reminded that this man's rage in battle was legendary. She shivered involuntarily.

'Well?' he prompted when she didn't answer.

She lifted her chin, her skin flushing. *Will he believe me?*

'I have never lain with a man.' *There, it is said. The shameful truth.*

He stared at her, his expression blank.

'Why?' he asked finally. *Does he believe me?*

She looked away, suddenly unable to bear the pressure of his gaze. 'I was afraid.' She felt less, somehow, for her shameful admission. She spoke softly to the goblet clutched in both hands.

She felt him sit up and reach for the goblet. He pried it from her fingers and put it aside with his. Then he forced her to look at him. 'Of what are you afraid?' he spoke calmly. There was a stillness to him as he asked.

She hesitated; *can I admit my deepest fear, to him of all people?* She licked her lips nervously. What should she say? Before she could formulate a plausible lie, he spoke with that harsh tone again, 'Do you prefer women? Is that it?'

She shook her head and her heart thumped. She swallowed.

'Are you malformed in some way?'

'No!'

He grunted, narrowing his eyes in thought, as if he were attempting to see right through her and reveal the deepest secrets of her heart.

'Did someone hurt you, make you afraid?' His voice cut across her panicked inner chatter. She looked away again, unable to bear his scrutiny. He seized her chin and forced her to look at him again. His expression was grim. He searched her face, for what she didn't know, finally, when he spoke, his voice was soft and low and it sent a shiver down her spine.

'I give you my word that you have nothing to fear from me. I will not hurt you in that way.'

What way? What does he think I meant? Her heart hammered. She swallowed and opened her mouth to ask and he drew her into his arms and kissed her. He was gentle at first, tender kisses on her lips and jaw, his hands held her, caressed her as if she was precious, fragile. She began to cling, her heart thundered, his mouth, his touch, ignited a fire in her blood, banishing panic, banishing her fear.

Rapidly, gentleness dissolved into possessive forceful kisses, he plundered her mouth and devoured her; his powerful arms surrounded her, his big hands callused and strong, stroking and squeezing her flesh with passionate ownership. His desire was a revelation. She was doing this to him. As much as he ignited her desire, she ignited his. She could sense his need in the power of his touch, in the shortness of his breath, see it in the fire in his eyes and feel it in the hard, hot flesh beneath his kilt. For the first time, she felt a different kind of power, the power of a woman over a man. Perhaps this was less of a surrender on her part, than she had thought and feared. She no longer cared that he would take her. She wanted him to. She moaned again, helpless to resist the ravenous desire low in her belly.

She became liquid with longing, as he bore her down onto the bed, crushing her with his big frame, his hands on her hot and urgent, his mouth demanding.

~*~

Her confession shook him and stirred a fierce protectiveness. Whoever had hurt her, made her afraid, if they still lived they would answer to him. For all her strength and outward mettle, she needed him. A warm glow in his chest bloomed with the thought. She needed him. Her small capable hands ran down his back as he pinned her soft yielding body to the bed with his weight. He kissed her deeply again and again, feeling her body arch under him, her mouth responding to his, their legs tangled. He stifled a groan, pulling back, striving for some sort of control.

He shifted on the bed, the soft mattress rustling beneath them, pressing her hand into the pillow above her head, palm to palm, fingers linked, as he bent to trace kisses down her jaw and nibble on the pulse in her neck. The ache in his groin urged him to remove her gown and take her with swift force, but her confession, her fear, made him hesitate, even as her little panting moans egged him on. *Such a contradiction. Afraid, yet so wildly responsive.*

He moved a hand up her thigh, pushing up her gown, sliding his fingers higher and finding her thighs well-oiled and slippery. His fingers slid higher still and found wet folds that revealed the full state of her arousal. *Holy Goddess.* He groaned, grinding his hard cock into her pelvis.

'Hathor…' He panted. He was hot, so hard he ached, his balls tight with need. 'Hathor?' It was a plea. He was begging her. He never begged. He reached for her gown. She smiled, answering his question. She wriggled free of the cloth as he lifted it over her head, her hands reaching for him, her eyes feverish with the same intensity and need as him. *Fear does not stop her now. Did she trick me? Does she lie? Goddess, I don't care.* He breathed fast, his pulse raced, he swallowed, his throat dry.

His eyes roamed over her body. Her beautiful breasts with perfect pink nipples pulled tight with her desire, her slender waist and the gentle curve of her hips, her triangle of red curls took his breath away. 'Goddess.' There was no other word for her. She was exquisite. He pulled the tie of his kilt and discarded it. He leaned over her, his cock a rampant red sword between them. She stared down at it, her legs splayed either side of him. The sight made him pulse with need to take her, fill her, own her, possess her. She lifted her head and stared up at him, her eyes wide; with fear? *No lie then.*

She reached up and brought him down on top of her, kissing him, pressing her body closer. *Ha! She is like me, willing to face fear head on and defeat it.* Admiration bloomed as his heart pumped and surged with a kind of possessive pride and fierce hunger.

He found her mouth and kissed her.

'Don't be afraid,' he whispered, moving his mouth to her ear, shifting his body into position. He moved his hips; the head of his cock encountered soft flesh and he gasped involuntarily with the shock of desire. He held still a moment as the pleasure pulsed through his body. He breathed out a muttered prayer beneath his breath. He moved again, probing further. More pulses of pleasure. *Goddess yes!* And sank inside her with a grunt that became a groan as her full glory engulfed his body. He buried his face in her neck and panted, almost overcome by the blissful sweet sharpness of her tight heat.

~*~

She held him to her, feeling him shake as his shaft slid into her. Her flesh gripped his and throbbed with pleasure. The Goddess had seized her; she was on the edge of release with just one thrust. She clutched at him; it felt so good, his body pressing her into the bed, filling her up, better than anything she had ever imagined. He began to move and her possessed body arced and vibrated with slippery, exquisite pleasure. She was close to breaking open. She panted and moaned and moved with him in a frantic pulsing seeking.

He thrust deep, hard and fast, his body was sheened in sweat and the perfumed oil of their conjoined skin. She pushed up against him as he plunged down, trying to pull him closer, deeper. Heat pulsed, convulsed between her legs. She felt the rushing pleasure arc through her like lightning in a thunderstorm, raging through her body and out the crown of her head and the soles of her feet. Glorious and swift and explosive—exquisitely, intensely pleasurable. She panted through it, feeling him shudder and grunt and groan out his own passion, a hot series of flooding shots inside her. *Goddess!*

He collapsed on her, heavy, still trembling, and she clung to him, shocked by the intensity and swiftness of their mutual release.

~*~

As the aftershocks ebbed and he got his breath back, a warmth pervaded his body, a peace that loosened his muscles and a sense of contentment enveloped him. He rolled sideways withdrawing from her body and pulling her closer with possessive joy. *She is mine.* She moved into his arms naturally, resting her head on his shoulder and she sighed.

'What is it?' He kissed the top of her head, sensitive to any possible discontent. *Did I hurt her?*

'Nothing. A silly fancy.' She traced her hand over his chest, over the tattoo of the black scorpion.

He captured her hand and kissed it. 'What?' He pressed, uncharacteristically anxious, wanting to know her thoughts, her feelings.

She bit her lip and looked up at him beneath her lashes. *Does she know how provocative that is? Does she know how beautiful she is?* He was sated, yet he wanted her all over again. His hand slid lazily down her side to caress her hip. He couldn't help himself. *I don't believe I will ever tire of touching her.*

'They say you are immune to the Scorpion's sting. Is it true?'

'Yes. I fell into a pit full of scorpions as a boy and got stung. Miraculously I survived. Scorpion stings are painful for me, but they won't kill me.'

'You *are* under the protection of the Goddess Serqet, then.'

'It seems so, yes. I have built a temple to her at Abdu, the place of my birth. I will take you there.' His thumb traced over her pelvis and she moved her hip, opening herself up to him. His cock pulsed in response. Her fear was banished. He smiled, pleased and wanting to please her. He bent forward to kiss her, his fingers traced over her mound to find the place of her pleasure.

In moments she was panting and moaning. He slid down her body, moving his mouth from her breasts to her belly to the moist heaven between her legs. She stared down at him, startled.

'What are you doing?'

He grinned and set to work to lick her to release. And soon he was hard enough to take her body a second time, with long deep thrusts, he held himself over her and watched her face as he brought her to release yet again.

'Oh Goddess,' she moaned, gasping and laughing, clenching on him. *Goddess, that is so good.* She brought her legs up and he lowered his weight and kissed her, thoroughly, deeply, roughly, his earlier gentleness forgotten. He wanted and he needed and he would have her. *She has possessed me.* He drove into her, hammered her into the mattress, hard, fast, panting, rapid pounding. Pleasure rose with each thrust, he would break with it, with the raging in his blood, his breath harsh, his pulse thundering. Hot pleasure. She writhed in his arms, panting, her nails grazed his skin, she groaned. He held her close, gripped her tight, drove himself deep and hard. She shuddered with desperate gasps. *Mine.* His body jerked, surrendered, pleasure exploded and seized his panting breath in a loud groan as he hit the apex of release and lost his seed in pulsing shots deep inside her. *Mine. Mine.*

He held her tight, feeling as if he had lost his sense of separateness. Even in prayer he had not felt this level of connectedness to another being. He lay perfectly still, listening to his own heartbeat, and felt himself in her, of her. It was extraordinary and precious. She clung to him and they breathed in unison, pulse and breath in sync. Gradually the feeling of absolute oneness subsided, leaving a warm comfort in its wake.

He moved his head and she looked at him, her expression dazed. He kissed her. A little while later they slowly disengaged and she curled into his arms, where she belonged. He stroked her and held her. He had found his home. It was in her. A fierce kind of pride and a recognition that this woman was the one he had waited all his life to meet took possession of his heart. A worthy partner and equal. *My Egypt. My woman. My Queen. My wife.*

~*~

He slept in her arms and she watched him until she needed to pass water. Returning to the bedside she found him awake and staring at her in the dark.

'Are you still afraid?'

'No.' She paused, she could let this go, but if she did she would be letting a lie sit between them. She took a breath and let it out slowly. 'I wasn't afraid of the act.'

He frowned puzzled. 'What then?'

'I was afraid that if a man took my body he would also take my power.' Admitting the truth, her fear, was suddenly easy.

The tension cleared and he smiled. It melted the harshness from his face and made him look younger and heartbreakingly handsome. Something inside her slipped and softened. She realised with dawning wonder, it was her heart.

'Very wise of you.' He drew her closer to the bed and kissed her fingers. It was such a strange gesture her mouth fell open in surprise. He dropped his gaze a moment and then looked at her sideways with that charming smile that melted her still further. 'I never thought I would meet a woman like you. We will be a formidable team, I think.'

She nodded, unsure how to respond to this.

'I will take your body, but not your power, Hathor. The Goddess lives in you, I can feel it. I will honour it. You will rule with me, beside me.'

'Thank you,' she whispered, feeling tears clog her throat. She never wept, not since her mother flew to heaven.

'I will protect you and the children you bear me with my last breath.'

She nodded again and slipped to her knees and bowed her head to him. 'I will always stand with you and serve you,' she spoke softly. The promise came from nowhere, but she meant it, with every fibre of her being. *This man is worthy of my service.* She knew it with the instinct that had guided her through the short, harsh years of her sole rule of Tarkhan.

'Thank you, my dear.' He drew her up into his arms and down onto the bed, where he kissed her again. A kiss that explored and invited. *We have a future, I know it.* She returned his kiss with her whole heart.

Colour my World
By
Lee-Ann Wallace

Ally turned the handle and pushed open the door. A bell jangled overhead.

It had taken six months and hundreds of dollars of phone credit to find this place. She stepped inside and closed the door. There was no waiting area, no booking desk, only an intimidating looking chair in the middle of the room and an old timber table pushed up against the wall, with a photocopy machine sitting on bricks beside it.

She lifted her sunnies and froze when she saw an A2-sized photo on the wall. She stood transfixed by the image of Cole Kingsley as he looked up from working on a client, his trademark wicked grin in place and tattoo machine in hand. Her heart fluttered as it always had, ever since she'd turned twelve and fallen in love with that grin.

But the blue eyes she'd loved so much weren't blue anymore. They were grey, like the rest of her world.

'You after some work?' a deep masculine voice asked.

Ally started, dropping her sunglasses back into place. She turned, her gaze landing on the man she'd come to see. Her eyes widened behind her glasses, her stomach flipping over. On second thought, she wanted to run—or throw up.

God, she'd forgotten how big he was, but he looked good. He'd been working out and there were tattoos on every inch of skin she could see except his face. The gangly teen and young man she'd grown up with had turned dangerously sexy.

Cole lifted one eyebrow and stared back at her.

Damn, she had to say something or she'd look like a nut case. He didn't seem to recognise her and she didn't blame him. The chubby country girl was gone and in her place was the person she'd become.

His gaze raked up and down her, only to come back to her face. Cole tilted his head to the side, in that sexy way that had made her breath catch before he'd left Ainsworth.

She'd left too, or been forced to. When they released her from the hospital, she'd had no reason to return to the town they'd both grown up in. Not without him there.

'I have a design I'd like done,' Ally said.

He raised one eyebrow and thrust his hand out. 'Give us a look then.'

Ally pulled a scroll of paper out of her bag.

Cole stalked forward and snatched it from her hand.

She gasped and stared up at him as he dragged the rubber band off and unrolled the paper.

Cole grunted as he looked down at her design. He turned it ninety degrees and rolled his lips together. 'Come back tomorrow. I'll start at seven in the morning.' He turned away without even looking at her and walked to the desk.

Ally watched him as he pulled out a piece of paper and started drawing. 'I, ah, thought the design was fine as it is,' she said.

He turned to look at her, his face hard. 'Do you want me to do it or not?'

She nodded. This was her only chance to fulfil her promise.

'Then you'll take what I draw, or I won't do it,' Cole said.

Ally swallowed. Cole had changed, but then so had she. 'Okay.'

~ * ~

A frigid wind blew down the street from the ocean when Ally opened the door to Cole's shop at seven the next morning. Cole was at the desk, papers spread out in front of him, a thick sweater covering all the tattoos she'd seen on him yesterday—except the ones creeping up his neck.

The little shop was warm, barely. There was a heater off to one side of the room. Cole didn't look up, didn't raise the pen he was drawing with, didn't acknowledge her presence in any way. She fidgeted and shifted from foot to foot. Should she let him know she was there? No, no, that was stupid. The bell above the door had rung. He knew she was there.

Ally looked around and walked over to a panel of black and grey designs on the wall. They were all Cole's designs. His signature was under every single one. Over half had *sold* written in red across them.

'Where do you want it?' Cole asked.

Ally jerked around at the unexpected question, her chest squeezing for a moment before it relaxed. 'On my side,' she replied.

He glanced at her. 'You had work done before?'

She shook her head.

Cole raised one eyebrow. 'It's gonna hurt like a bitch. I can do it on your thigh. It won't hurt so much there.'

Ally shook her head again. 'No, I want it on my side. I know it hurts more there. Everyone said I should get something smaller, but I don't want anything else.'

'Suit yourself, but I'm not stopping once I start.' He turned away without waiting for her to respond, a look on his face she couldn't interpret.

He wasn't anything like the man she remembered, but then it had been eight years since she'd seen him last.

Cole stood and his chair screeched across the tile floor. He slapped a drawing down on the photocopy machine and slammed the lid closed. 'Get your gear off. I need to see if it'll fit.'

Ally hesitated before she dropped her bag on the floor and stripped off her jumper. Her long sleeve t-shirt followed, then her singlet. She piled her clothes on top of her bag and walked over to stand behind Cole in her bra and jeans.

Her stomach twisted, a pain squeezing her chest tight. It didn't matter what he thought of her. She was here to get a tattoo, and if the thought of someone seeing her partly undressed freaked her out? Well, she'd better learn to deal with it.

Cole turned back, a piece of paper in his hand and froze. He stared at her stomach and side. 'This isn't going to cover all those scars, little girl. I can make it bigger if you want.'

'I don't want to cover the scars,' Ally said, her chest loosening a little. 'I want it on the other side.'

He grunted and sat in the chair. 'I may have long arms, but they aren't that long, sweetheart. Come over here.'

Ally gaped at him for a second. His entire demeanour had changed. Gone was the gruff, impatient man and in its place was the Cole she remembered. She walked forwards and turned side on.

Warm hands gripped her, and he guided her between his parted legs.

A breath shuddered out of her, everything low down inside clenching at the brush of his fingers against her bare skin.

Cole held the paper up against her side, smoothing edges into place and tilting his head this way and that. He sat back, the design in his hand.

'Right. It fits nice. I'll need to draw a bit to make it look right. If you like it when I get it on you, it will take about twelve hours to finish. I can do it all in one go, but seeing as it's your first, we should split it up into three sessions. It'll be two hundred an hour. I expect half up front and half at the end.'

Ally stared at him. He was giving her a discount. Everyone told her to expect four hundred an hour, double what everyone else charged.

'I can do it in one session,' Ally said. 'I have a high tolerance for pain, and I have the cash in my bag. I can pay you now if you want.'

Cole stared at her for so long Ally thought he wasn't going to respond. His pale blue eyes sucked her in and dragged her into the past, into a place where she'd been happy, loved, and colour had filled her world, Cole had filled her world.

Now the world was shades of grey and black, and red was the only colour Ally saw. And now blue.

'Let's get started then,' Cole said.

~ * ~

Ally stood in front of Cole, her jeans shoved down her hips and her singlet bunched up and taped in place to the underside of her breast. He smoothed the stencil over her wet skin sticking it in place and easing the edges around her slight curves.

Cole's touch was doing things to her insides, making her feel things she hadn't felt in so long she'd started to believe all she'd ever done was imagine them. Every time she looked at him and caught his gaze the blue of his eyes startled her.

She'd remembered his blue eyes, but not what shade they'd been. She'd thought they were sky blue, but the sky had been grey for so long she'd forgotten what it looked like too.

He peeled the paper from her, leaving dark lines on her pale skin, and sat back. He looked over the design, his lower lip caught between his teeth. He'd done that before too. It was his thinking face, and she'd found him looking at her like that a lot before everything went to hell.

Ally turned away before she blurted out who she was and asked him if he remembered her. It didn't matter. She was here to fulfil the promise she'd made to him.

When you make pictures on people's skin, Cole, I want you to make one on mine.

By the time you're old enough, Ally, you will have forgotten.

I won't. I'll never forget, Cole. I promise. Nobody will ever draw on me 'cept you.

Ally jerked at the touch of something cold on her skin. She looked down to find Cole with a pen poised over her skin.

'You good?' he asked his gaze on her.

'Yeah.'

He looked down, and the pen touched her skin again.

Ten minutes later Cole turned her to the mirror and showed her what he'd done. Ally stared at the dark lines on her side and tried to see what it would look like when he'd filled it with black, shades of grey, and splashes of red.

The cat was there in the foreground, and the crown rolling away down an alley, both from her original drawing, but there were so many more little details. A word here and there, lines that branched out seeming to have no purpose, but without them, she knew the design would look sparse and unfinished. And one little phrase almost hidden amongst other things.

A cat and a king went out one day…

Ally's breath caught. Oh god! Did he know? She didn't dare turn and look at him, couldn't bear to see what was on his face. Anger, rejection, or even hatred.

'It's perfect,' she said.

She couldn't stop her gaze from lifting and meeting Cole's in the mirror, but he wasn't looking at her, he was looking at a scar on her back she'd kept hidden from him. Her brother's initials, branded in her skin.

~ * ~

The buzz of Cole's machine almost drowned out the low hum of the radio he'd put on and much to Ally's surprise, he worked in silence. After he'd seen the scar on her back, he'd turned away and had said nothing since, except curt directions.

Her body hummed, not only from the constant rush of endorphins but from arousal. It left her uncomfortable and throbbing between her legs, a light sweat covering her.

Ally had blocked out the pain after about half an hour, but she couldn't block out the pain of knowing this was the one and only time she'd get to feel Cole's hands on her. She'd never again get to feel the slide of his fingers as he rubbed ointment onto her skin, or the light pressure he used to make her roll this way or that. Once she was gone, he'd forget about her, and she would never see him again.

It was for the best, she was sure. Seeing her scar had changed something. The Cole she remembered was gone again, but he'd remained gentle as if he was afraid of breaking her.

He lifted his machine and wiped away the excess ink. She could see him in the mirror hanging on the wall. He had that look on his face again, his teeth biting his lower lip and a deep frown marring his brow.

The buzzing stopped, and he blew out a breath. His machine landed with a clatter on the metal cart he'd pulled out of a back room.

Cole squirted liquid all over the tattoo, the excess dribbling down her front and back to soak into the paper under her. He wiped her down, his strokes gentle on her raw skin.

'I'll tape you up as best I can,' he said. 'Are you staying in town?'

'Yeah,' Ally replied. 'I have a room at Mac's Hotel for a week.'

He grunted, then said, 'You'll need to wash it in an hour. Body wash is fine. Leave the cover on until then, and take some more painkillers before you sleep. I want you to come back before you leave, and I'll check how it's healing.'

Cole was all business as he showed her the finished piece in the mirror, then applied an ointment and taped thin plastic in place.

Ally fixed her clothes and shoved her bra in her bag. She pulled out the envelope with the second half of the money to pay Cole.

Should she say something before she left? Ally shook her head. No, it was better she paid him and left. Cole had a life here.

He didn't need her bringing up a past he'd left behind. He didn't need to know what had happened after he'd left.

A door slammed somewhere out the back and Ally jerked. Cole stalked through the door and shoved the desk chair out of the way with such force it toppled over and crashed to the floor.

'It took half an hour less than I expected, so you owe me eleven hundred.'

She sucked in a breath. Something had happened between him finishing and now, but she didn't dare ask what. Ally counted out the money onto the desk. Eleven crisp one hundred dollar bills. She folded the envelope in half and shoved it in her back pocket.

'Thank you.' She turned away towards the door. 'It's everything I could have wished for and more.' She glanced at him, her hand on the door to find Cole's eyes boring into her.

His eyes weren't blue after all. They were a stormy grey, like the clouds that had built up during the day and now soaked the narrow streets of Scott's Bay.

He didn't say a word as she opened the door and stepped out into the freezing rain.

~ * ~

Ally peeled the tape from her skin. Rich red blood coated the inside of the plastic Cole had taped to her. She tamped down the rising panic and breathed in through her nose and out through her mouth.

It was a little blood, nothing more. Once she washed and put on the cream the bleeding would stop. Her hands shook as she reached for her bottle of body wash and the hotel's face-washer.

She wet the cloth in the basin full of warm water and squeezed it over her new tattoo. The water sluiced over her skin and ran down her body to stain her white panties a rich pink.

A sad little cat
Went out one day
Over the hills and far away

Ally squeezed her eyes shut. Not now, not now.

Thumping on the hotel room door made her jump and cut through the taunting voice running through her mind. She blew a breath out through pursed lips and pushed away the thoughts in her mind like the psychiatrist had taught her.

She threw the washer in the sink and walked on shaky legs to the door. The safety chain rattled as she slid it along its little track and Ally yanked the door open.

'You ordered room serv—holy shit, did Cole do that?'

Ally frowned at the teenage boy standing in front of her door with a tray in his hands. She glanced down at herself. 'Yes, Cole did it. Thank you for bringing my food.'

'Oh, no worries, lady. The colours look awesome by the way.'

She took her tray and shut the door, returning to the bathroom to wash Cole's work.

Ally stared at her new tattoo in the mirror. The teen must have been mistaken, there was only one colour other than black that Cole had put in her tattoo: red.

~ * ~

Cole's little bell jangled when Ally pushed open his door the day she was due to leave. She had packed her car and handed in her room key.

She had no idea where she was going next or what she was going to do. She hadn't thought that far. Her one and only goal since they'd released her from the hospital had been to find Cole and fulfil her promise. Now she'd done that, but she couldn't make up her mind what she wanted to do next.

Cole looked up from his desk. 'Get your gear off. I can't see through clothes.'

Ally swallowed at his sharp tone, tears stinging her eyes. She missed the old Cole, and she didn't know how to make things right.

Ally stripped off her long sleeve t-shirt and held it and her bag in one hand. She walked forward and stopped right in front of Cole, so there was no need for him to touch her.

He studied his work and grunted. 'Looks good. It's healing well. The shading and colour look even, so it shouldn't need touching up unless you ever want a refresh.'

She stepped away and pulled her shirt over her head. 'Okay, I'll remember that. Thank you.'

'Are you heading home now?'

Cole's question seemed innocent enough, but an underlying anger coloured his words.

Ally dragged in a breath and turned away before he saw the tears gathering in her eyes. 'I don't have a home,' she whispered and strode for the door.

Heavy footsteps rushed after her and Cole's hand slammed against the door, stopping Ally from opening it. 'Is that it, alley cat? You're gonna waltz in here like you have no idea who I am and leave again? Why did you even come if that's all you're going to do?'

She choked back a sob at hearing him use the nickname he'd given her. 'I made you a promise, and it seemed like the most important thing to do after...' She sucked in a breath. 'You don't want me here, Cole. All I can do is remind you of bad memories.'

'Don't tell me what I want, Ally. Do you have a man?'

Hot tears spilled over at the fury in his voice and ran in silent trails down her cheeks. The first tears she'd cried in six years. 'I've never had a man.'

Cole was silent for so long Ally didn't think he was going to say anything, but when he did, his voice was the same soft voice he'd used all those years ago.

'Do you still love me, alley cat?'

A fist squeezed Ally's heart and stole her voice. All she could manage was a shaky nod. He grabbed her arm and locked the door, then pulled her with a gentle but firm grip, through his shop and up a set of stairs at the back, to a studio apartment on the second floor. He ushered her over to the huge bed and coaxed her to sit on the edge.

Ally clutched her bag in two hands so tight her knuckles protested and avoided Cole's gaze. She didn't want to see his eyes grey, she wanted them to be blue as they had been before.

Cole dropped to his knees in front of her and settled his backside down on his heels. He braced his hands on either side of her hips, his long fingers pressing into the covers with alarming force.

'I'm only going to give you one chance, Ally. If you choose me, I won't ever let you go again. I don't know what happened after I left, but from your scars, it wasn't good. Sweetheart, look at me.'

She turned her still damp gaze on Cole, and a small sound escaped her. Blue eyes gazed back at her.

'I love you, alley cat. Will you stay here with me and be mine?' Cole asked.

Ally stared down at him her eyes wide. He still loved her, after all this time. In the months that she was searching for him, she never imagined he'd still want her, still love her. If it hadn't been the memories she had of him, she would never have survived, and now he was giving her everything she hadn't dared to want. 'Yes, Cole Kingsley. I'll be yours.'

~ * ~

Cole hung his head and blew out a breath, then he surged up and pressed his lips to hers. Ally gasped, her lips parting when Cole's met hers.

He tasted like fresh mint and the soft slide of his tongue against hers sent a cascade of heat shooting through her. She'd dreamed of kissing Cole once upon a time. But none of her fantasies could have prepared her for the devastation he would wreak with one simple kiss.

He ripped his lips from hers and demanded, 'How sore are you?'

She shook her head. 'I'm not. I don't feel much pain

anymore.'

Cole stared back at her, one brow raised. 'We're going to talk about that later. Right now, I need to be in you.'

Ally's eyes popped wide, and her lips parted. She swiped her tongue along her lower one and whispered, 'Okay.'

Cole grinned at her with that wicked expression that never failed to make her insides squirm. He reached for the hem of his jumper and stripped it off.

Ally gasped at the sheer volume of tattoos covering his thickly muscled chest and arms. A surge of heat shot through her and her insides clenched dragging a little sound of shock from her.

Cole's gaze snapped to hers.

Heat washed over Ally's face and she looked away.

A low chuckle made her face flame hotter. 'Alley cat, don't feel embarrassed that you find me attractive. I spent the whole day working on you with a hard-on. Why do you think I was so pissed when you left?'

Ally's eyes widened, and she turned back to him, the clench of her inner muscles making her throb. The thought of Cole aroused made her feel warm and damp.

He tugged the bag from her fingers and dropped it on the floor beside the bed, then cupped her face, his big hands warm on her cool skin, and his blue gaze exactly as she remembered.

'Welcome home, alley cat,' he murmured, then he kissed her again.

Tears stung Ally's eyes, but before she could become overwhelmed by her emotions Cole started stripping her of her clothes. He pressed her onto the bed until she lay back, her mind in a whirl and her gaze locked on him.

His belt buckle clinked as he undid it and the rasp of his zipper sent a spasm through her. He lifted his gaze to hers and pushed his jeans and jocks down his thighs in one swift movement.

Ally couldn't have stopped her gaze from following Cole's hands if her life depended on it. At the sight of his straining arousal, she sucked in a breath until her lungs couldn't hold any more air. Her mind froze, and before she could gather her thoughts, Cole climbed on the bed with her.

He gripped her ankles and pushed her feet towards her bottom, a small packet between his teeth. When he'd settled with his knees open on either side of her hips, he lifted each of her feet and placed one on either side of his thighs. He tossed the small packet from his mouth onto the bed and rested his hands on her knees.

He lifted his gaze to hers, his beautiful eyes the only thing she could see, and asked, 'Do you trust me, Ally?'

She nodded. That had never been in question. She wouldn't have sought him out to keep her promise if she hadn't trusted him.

'Then I want you to spread your legs and keep your hands flat on the bed.'

A low flush heated her cheeks, but she did what he asked. She panted, her body betraying how he'd made her feel with all his kisses. Ally watched Cole through slitted eyes as he raked his gaze down her from neck to her exposed sex and back again.

He braced himself over her with his hands on either side of her shoulders and leant down until they were almost nose to nose. 'I'm going to touch you, alley cat. If I do something you don't like, promise you'll tell me, and for fuck's sake, don't let me hurt you.'

'I won't, I promise, Cole.'

He caught her up in a kiss that rocked the foundations of her soul. Cole teased and tempted, nibbled at her lips and stroked her tongue with his. He stroked her arms and teased her breasts, rubbing his thumbs over her tight nipples until Ally felt like she might die. He teased her with blunt nails down her ribcage, avoiding her new tattoo, on his way to her belly and thighs.

She whimpered when his hand skated close to the thatch of hair between her legs, then away again. Closer, then away again. He changed directions and stroked up the inside of her thighs making her tremble in anticipation.

Ally's hips jerked when his finger finally stroked in a soft touch over the sensitive skin between her legs. Her hands spasmed and she gripped the coverlet tight.

A low groan rumbled out of Cole and he ripped his mouth from hers. 'You're so wet, alley cat.' He slid his finger upwards and stroked her clitoris, sending a jolt through her.

Ally whimpered, the sound pulled from her against her will, and her back arched, her fingers clenched in the coverlet to stop her from reaching for him. She needed… something, something that was out of her reach, that she couldn't quite grasp.

Cole slipped his finger down again and pressed inwards, invading a part of her that had never felt the touch of a man.

Ally's back arched, her hips lifting off the bed, and she cried out, 'Cole!'

'Fuck, baby, are you coming already?'

She whimpered, her body trembling uncontrollably as wave after wave of sensation washed through her centred around Cole's finger sliding in and out of her.

A tearing sound broke the spell Cole had woven around her and Ally opened her eyes to find him opening the small packet with his teeth. She watched him roll a condom down the length of his arousal, her mind in a complete daze.

Cole slipped his finger from her and Ally moaned at the empty feeling he left behind, but he shifted, the swirling designs of his black and grey tattoos rippling as he pulled her closer with a firm grip on her hips.

Ally's eyes widened as he pressed in and filled her, his gaze locked with hers. She gasped, and whimpered, 'Cole.'

He groaned. 'Fuck, you're tight.'

Her breath locked in her throat, her eyelids fluttering shut when Cole swivelled his hips, withdrawing a little and surging back inside. Ally's thighs trembled, her hips lifting off the bed. Everything inside her tightened.

Cole shifted his hips again and Ally gasped in a breath. Her thighs tensed and tingles spread up her legs from her toes.

'Fuck, alley cat.' Cole groaned and pulled out, only to slam all the way into her.

No one had ever said sex would feel like this. Her whole world centred around having Cole inside her and what he was making her feel. Ally whimpered as his rhythm sped, every stroke ripping a little cry from her.

Ally bucked, sucked in a breath, her hands gripped the coverlet tight, and she cried out as she shattered for the man she loved.

Cole grunted, then cursed. He slammed in and shuddered,

his hands gripping her hips tight.

~ * ~

Ally opened her eyes to find Cole bathed in colour. Tears stung as she drank in the rich brown of his hair, the light golden tan of his skin, and the riot of colour that covered his body.

Her tears turned into a flood as emotion finally overwhelmed her.

Cole gathered her close. 'Shhh, Ally, it's okay.'

A sob ripped through her chest and she wrapped her arms around him, clinging to the man who had been her only friend and the memory that had kept her alive.

'I missed you,' she choked out.

'I know, baby.' He squeezed her tighter. 'I missed you, too.'

Ally swallowed. She had to tell him, she had to tell him all of it. 'I lost my colours after you left. Then everything turned red, so much red, and I hated it. But red was the colour that set me free.'

She looked up into the dazzling blue of his eyes. 'But you gave me back my favourite colour, you gave me blue, and now you've given me everything. You've coloured my world, Cole.'

He frowned down at her. He didn't understand, but that was okay. In a soft voice, Ally started to sing.

'A sad little cat
Went out one day
Over the hills and far away
The cat said,
"King, where are you?"'

And Cole Kingsley replied, 'Right here by your side, alley cat, where I should have been all along.'

The Girl with the Spiderweb Tattoo
By
Wren St. Claire

Monday

She was definitely not his type.

She had black and crimson spiky hair; black eye makeup, lipstick and nails; studs in her ears, nose and eyebrow; and wore a short, short black pleated tunic over a white high-necked blouse; and pair of doc martens. Classic punk-goth. Not his type at all. Not that he was in the market anyway. His fiancée, Lindsay, would have his balls on a platter.

The software program that created spider diagrams had failed to load properly and he'd put in a call to the Help Desk. He needed the app for a report, due at five. And Shelley showed up to fix the problem.

'Hey,' she said, leaning in the doorway of his office.

He looked up from the spreadsheet he was working on.

He'd seen Shelley around the office at a distance but this was the first time he'd seen her up close. She smiled and he noticed that her eyes were blue. 'Your computer's not playing nice with the app loader, I hear.' She straightened up and came into his office.

He nodded, trying to place her accent. English maybe? She came around his desk and he scooted back to let her in. Those blue eyes danced over him and she grinned. What made her smile, he hadn't a clue. He pushed his glasses up his nose.

'I'm Shelley, by the way.' She stuck out her hand and he took it. 'Reynold, isn't it?' Her hands were small and slender, like the rest of her. Up close she was kind of cute, despite the accessories.

'Nice to meet you.' He recovered his hand.

She cocked her head to one side and her smile widened. He was amusing her, and he didn't have a clue why. 'May I?' She gestured at his computer.

'Sure.' He scooted back further and she leaned over his keyboard and began typing. Her nails clicked rapidly over the keys, but the sight of her bare legs, pert bottom and the glimpse of white cotton nickers under her very short skirt distracted his attention. *White cotton?* He swallowed, a rush of heat racing up his body. He shifted in his seat, reaching up to loosen his collar. She turned, leaning back against his desk return, and pursed her lips knowingly. She knew he'd been looking.

'Log back in.' She waved at the keyboard.

He avoided her gaze, trying for cool and failing. He scooted forward and logged in, his fingers trembling slightly. She leaned over and pointed at the start menu, he caught a whiff of lilac talc. 'Your app should be here.' Her neck stretched and he caught a glimpse of a thin black line at a forty-five degree angle with two others, like fins, coming off either side of it peeking out of the white collar. *A tattoo?*

He used the mouse to find the app and bingo, there it was. His pulse beat in his fingertips as he clicked and it loaded. He smiled. 'Thanks.'

'You're welcome.' She jumped off his desk. She seemed to do everything with a bounce. He watched her move towards the door, strangely reluctant to let her go. As if feeling his gaze, she turned back, leaning on the doorframe. 'You going to the work Christmas party?'

'Ah, no. I have a dinner at my fiancée's parents on Friday night.'

'Oh.' She shrugged, her sparkle quashed. 'Have a good one.'

'You too,' he said automatically, watching her walk away. *Did she just hit on me?*

~*~

Friday

The IT guys were being juvenile with the balloons and helium gas, and they thought they were hilarious. Shelley cracked an icy cold Corona, walking away from her embarrassing colleagues. It was early and the party hadn't really started yet. The band was still setting up and the caterers were laying out drinks and food. The top floor of their building that housed the executive suites and board room, plus a huge balcony with views of the river and city, was the only space big enough to contain the fifteen hundred strong staff of Lord & Timson, one of the biggest accounting firms in Brisbane.

Staff were trickling in from their floors and grabbing drinks. Shelley wandered about sipping her beer and watching. Her contract had just been extended for another six months if she wanted to stay and she was still trying to decide if that was what she wanted. She hadn't made a lot of friends, but then she didn't need them. Doing her own thing was what Shelley did best; she'd made a career of that. People judged her by the way she looked and she liked it that way. It told her exactly where she stood with them.

Propping herself against a wall, she watched the band testing their sound equipment. The drummer was kind of cute, all lean muscles and tatts. But then she noticed the lead singer, a tall redhead in distressed jeans and a diamanté-studded bra. They were an item, she could tell by the body language as they talked. And sure enough, the conversation concluded and they exchanged a quick kiss before the woman wandered back to the mike stand at the front of the stage. Shelley suppressed a sigh. Were all the cute guys taken? A little action tonight would be welcome; it had been a long time between drinks.

Doing guys from the office was a bad idea in principle, but provided they were prepared to accept that it was a one-off it would be okay. The last thing she wanted was a relationship. She'd travelled from the other side of the globe to get away from that.

Pity that guy from accounting was taken: Reynold. She'd do him in a heartbeat. Had there been chemistry there? She licked her lips, remembering lean muscles that even a business shirt couldn't hide, with that dark hair, pale skinned Celtic look she couldn't resist and gorgeous, dark-lashed green eyes behind his goofy glasses. And so straight, you'd have to stick his finger in a light socket to get him to admit he had a pulse. Except he'd never go for a girl like her. Although he *had* looked at her bottom when she'd stuck it in his face. He'd blushed. So cute. And so irresistible to tease.

Fiancée. Bet she was the twinset and pearls type, Miss Goodie-Two-Shoes. Poor guy; in ten or so years he was going to hit forty and wonder where his life went. Wife, mortgage, two point five kids and middle aged spread. *Boring!*

Shelley drained her beer bottle and pushed herself off the wall. Maybe there'd be some more interesting prospects on the balcony.

She headed over to the drinks table, dropping her empty in one of the bins provided, and stopped dead as Mr Spider-Diagram-App himself turned away from the drinks table in her direction. Reynold. *What is he doing here?* He had a beer in his hand and he was staring straight at her. He'd ditched his glasses. She smiled and moved towards him.

'Hey, I thought you had a date with the future parents-in-law?'

He'd removed his tie and loosened his collar. She realised with a shock he looked tired and a bit haggard. There was a heaviness around his eyes and despite his attempt to smile, he looked sad. *What happened since Monday?*

'Change of plans,' he said taking a generous swig of his beer. His shoulders were tight and his jaw set. Angry tension. That hadn't been there on Monday. He stared at her as if bringing her into focus. 'Sorry. My manners are shot. Would you like a drink?'

'Yes, please. Corona.'

He turned back to the drinks table and opened a bottle for her. She took it and they clinked bottles.

'I was heading for the balcony.' She turned and he followed her lead across the room to the big glass doors that opened onto the sweeping balcony. The sun was still up, but heading towards the horizon with blazing glory. It had been a hot day and was still warm. Resting her elbows on the balcony, she pretended to admire the view of the river while checking him out.

He leaned beside her staring at the river, his expression sombre.

'What's up?' she asked.

~*~

Reynold started, realising he'd lapsed into a funk again. He shouldn't have come. 'Sorry—'

'Stop apologising. What's the matter?'

'Ah!' He rubbed a hand through his hair. 'You sure you want to know?' *Do I want to talk about this?*

'Yes, or I wouldn't have asked.'

Yeah, he wanted to tell someone. He hadn't even told his parents yet. 'I found out on Tuesday that Lindsay's in love with another guy. I'm still trying to process it.' *There, it's out there, and it's real and you're such a loser.*

'That's your fiancée?'

He nodded, feeling a kind of relief in sharing.

'You dumped her arse?' she asked bluntly.

He looked at her, startled by the expression and felt the first urge to laugh since Tuesday. 'Um, yes.'

'Good.' She sipped her beer. 'She wasn't right for you anyway.'

'You don't know the first thing about her—or me for that matter.' *How would you know that?*

'I know she wasn't into you or she wouldn't have fallen for another guy. And I know more about you than you think.' Her charcoal smudged eye shadow and thick mascara made her eyes bigger.

'What do you know?' Shelley was the most unusual girl he'd ever met—direct almost to the point of rudeness. It was kind of refreshing. He kind of liked it.

Her blood red lipstick smile was wicked. His pulse jumped. 'I know what turns you on.' She turned towards him and ran her tongue over her lower lip. *That* was wicked-sexy.

A rush of heat went through his body, like an electric shock. His heart pounded and the heat pooled in his groin. The fog that had possessed him for the last four days lifted and he finally looked at her properly for the first time that night. She was wearing a short, tight-fitting black lace dress that clung to her slender shape. The dress had an uneven hemline, which finished above a pair of thigh-high black boots with wicked stiletto heels.

A delicate spider web tattoo was inked on the side of her neck.

She was stunning. Alluring. Definitely sexy. *And hitting on me?*

She laid a hand over his on the balcony and a tingle zapped straight from her touch to his groin. His brain melted. He turned his hand under hers and clasped it. She stared up at him with those large smoky blue eyes. She squeezed his hand and her touch sent another jolt through his body. *What the fuck?*

She leaned in and stretched up to whisper in his ear. 'Follow me.'

She turned and walked away. He watched her. His body was vibrating, literally. He'd never felt anything like this before. A surge of achy longing made him move. He followed her, a pulse in his neck and his groin that he couldn't ignore.

She went back through the glass doors and threaded her way across the now crowded and noisy room. He followed until she reached a side door and used a swipe card to open it. He caught up with her as she passed through the door, catching it before it closed in his face. He followed her into the wood panelled corridor. They were in the executive suite. She reached another door, swiped it and pushed it open. This time she paused and looked back over her shoulder. He reached out and caught the door. She leaned against it. The spotlight above her head illuminated the spider web tattoo on her pale smooth skin. He caught a whiff of lilac talc, the scent and heat from her body, pulled him in. He leaned forward and she ducked under his arm and slipped into the room. He followed, letting the door shut behind him.

They were in an office—one of the Exec's but he was too fuddled to work out which one. The sun had gone down now and the lights of the city and the river were visible through the window, the room lit primarily by the dim night light. Everything was shadowy and intimate. It was a large and well-appointed room with a big rosewood desk, an imposing chair and a couch. Each piece of furniture sparked wicked potential. The muffled sound of the band starting up and the thump of the base came through the wall, but they were alone.

His breath hitched and his dick lengthened. Had she really brought him here to seduce him? *Fuck*, the thought made him ache. A week ago this would have been unimaginable. It was crazy. But this week had been crazy. His world had been turned upside down and suddenly this freaky-sexy girl wanted him?

He moved towards her. She had stopped in front of the desk and turned to face him. He reached out and put an arm around her waist, pulling her into him. She put a hand on his chest, but not to push him away. He could feel the heat of her palm through his shirt. *She wants this? Wants me?*

His arm tightened around her and he touched her face with his other hand. He stared into her eyes, dark in the dim light, listening to them both breathing, feeling his heart beating. He had never felt so alive, so present, as he did in this moment. His skin tingled with awareness of her, of her other hand, mirroring his, touching his face. He slid his hand to the nape of her neck, cradling her skull, pushing his fingers through her short hair and lowering his head until his mouth hovered just over hers, anticipating the moment. He hadn't kissed another woman in five years—not since he'd gotten serious with Lindsay. And he hadn't had sex in over three months. That should have warned him something was wrong. How could he have been so blindsided? *Stop thinking. You have a gorgeous girl here offering you heaven. Remember what that feels like?*

Finally he closed that fractional gap between their mouths, her lips grazed his and a tingling explosion of pleasurable heat coursed through his body. His arm pulled her tighter against him and he kissed her, pulled into the seductive pleasure of her mouth.

It was intoxicating, more achingly wonderful than he could ever recall a kiss being before. She slanted her head and parted her lips and he dipped between them with his tongue; she widened her mouth to him. She was slender and soft and absolutely delicious. He was hard, achingly hot and hard. *Oh fuck I want you!* He kissed her and kissed her again, devouring her mouth until they were both panting.

Slow down! Breathe!

His mouth moved to her jaw and his hand to her breast; his fingers traced the line of flesh above the lace of her dress. *Is she really going to let me do this?* He pushed the strap off her shoulder and slid his hand under the lace to cup her breast and fondle her nipple. She hummed appreciation, which kicked up his pulse and made his cock twitch and leak. He was shaking.

He found her mouth again. God he'd never kissed like this, so ravenously hungry. His other hand moved downward to grasp that pert little bottom he'd tried not to look at on Monday when she cheekily thrust it in his face. She wriggled against him, rubbing on his now raging erection and nipped his lower lip. He groaned, pressing her closer.

He pulled back a fraction to catch his breath and she reached up to unbutton his shirt, smiling that wicked sexy smile that set his pulses racing. A sudden thought crashed through his lust ridden senses and he grabbed her hands as she reached the fourth button of his shirt.

'Protection.'

_~*~

Shelley reached for the small shoulder bag she had dropped on the desk. She pulled out a strip of three condoms. 'I'm a girl scout.' She grinned.

So she came prepared to have sex with someone. ¬Don't over think it Rey. It's you she's chosen. Don't disappoint her.

Like I did Lindsay?

Shut the fuck up!

He swallowed, closing his eyes reflexively in an attempt to shut off that train of thought.

'Hey.' He felt her hand brush his face. Her voice was soft, low, husky. 'Forget her.'

He opened his eyes. 'What¬?'

'I'm psychic,' she said with that grin, touching his lip with her thumb. She scanned his face with her eyes, a question in them. A fleeting doubt. 'Do you want this?'

God yes!

Time to be as blunt as she was. He cupped her face in his hands, letting himself drown in her eyes. 'I want you. I want to be inside you.' He watched her flush and her eyes catch fire as he said it. God, he was going to combust with desire. 'I want to lay you down on that desk and fuck you.'

'Do it,' she whispered, reaching for his shirt and pulling it from his pants, undoing the last couple of buttons, then moving to his trousers while her mouth kept his busy with more delicious, ravenous kisses.

He ran his hands down her hips over the lace and squeezed her bottom. *Is she wearing a g-string?* He couldn't feel any underwear. He reached for the hem of the skirt and hitched it up, running his hands up bare warm flesh.

'Fuck, Shelley!' he muttered, looking down to confirm his suspicion. She was bare beneath her dress. The knowledge galvanised him into action. He couldn't wait another second. He lifted her onto the desk and she fumbled for the strip of condoms. She ripped one open and with trembling fingers, lined it up on the head of his twitching, aching cock and dressed him in one slick movement of her hand. *Jeezus!* His hips jerked with the heat of her touch and he groaned. She lay back, lifting her knees and smiling up at him with feverish desire in her eyes.

Holding her hips, he shifted and with one quick thrust he was in heaven. He closed his eyes and breathed as the fire shot through his body, fighting for some sort of control.

Having mastered the urge to come on the spot, he opened his eyes and leaned over her, staring into her eyes as he began to thrust. Slow, deep, hard thrusts. She met each with a twist of her hips and a little grunt of satisfaction. He sped up gradually, unable to stop now. Her grunts became gasps as her hands grabbed at him and she bit his shoulder. Her boot-clad legs wrapped around him. Her body writhed under and around him and he moved one hand down to hold her hip while he braced himself on the desk to get a better angle and thrust hard and fast. A rapid, pounding rhythm, building, building... She jack-knifed under him and moaned; he felt her pleasure break in the trembling of her body and the keening cry in his ear. The pull of it was too much to resist.

Exquisite pleasure hit, sharp as a papercut, electrifying his nerve endings and shuddering through his body. Impossible to stop, the wave engulfed him and exploded with breath-robbing intensity. He groaned as the lightning struck deep inside, set fire to his balls and boiled out his cock in pulsing jets that poleaxed him with their intensity. He shuddered and shook and collapsed on her as the aftershocks rumbled and settled and he was finally still. Sweat congealing on his skin, breathing hard, pulse heavy and slowing.

He became gradually aware of her lips on his jaw and her hands stroking his sweat slicked skin under his shirt. He lifted his head and stared down into her face. She was flushed and her eyes glowed. A soft smile curved her blood red lips.

'I knew you'd be a good fuck.' Her voice was husky, languorous.

Startled, he laughed. 'Since when?'

'The moment I saw you three months ago.' She traced a finger down his jaw. 'You didn't see me. I was setting up a computer for a new staff member on your floor and I saw you leave your office and walk over to the printer. I kept hoping you'd need some IT help, but you never called the help desk until Monday.'

'I did see you,' he admitted.

'Did you? What did you think?' She watched his face and he got the feeling the question was more than casual curiosity.

'I thought you were probably cute under all the Goth get up, but it was hard to tell.'

'But you never envisaged yourself with someone who looks like me?'

'Until now, no.' *But then I didn't envisage Lindsay cheating on me either.*

'How do you feel now?' she asked, cocking her head to the side. The action exposed the spider web tattoo on her neck and his eyes were drawn to it, fascinated. He'd never fucked a woman with a tattoo before.

'Like I could conquer the world. Thank you.' He gently kissed her blood red mouth. 'It was wonderful.'

He shifted and, anchoring the condom, pulled out. There was a box of tissues on the desk and he used them to ball up the condom and dropped it in the bin.

Shelley sat up on her elbows, her skirt hitched up round her waist, her legs dangling. She had a neatly trimmed curly bush; the sight gave him a residual thrill. He could do her again, maybe from behind?

This should be the awkward bit. But she didn't seem

bothered. Instead she looked relaxed and sexy. Would she be up for seconds? Better not push his luck. He pulled up his jocks, pants and the zip, but didn't bother with the buttons. She didn't seem in a hurry to pull her dress down. She was watching him, amused. Why did he amuse her? It was vaguely unsettling.

His eyes strayed back to the tattoo. Its delicate dark lines were just visible in the dim light and unable to resist it any longer, he leaned over to touch the delicate pattern with the tip of his tongue. She sighed and stretched her neck further to give him better access. He traced the pattern with his finger and then licked her skin and sucked on it gently. She moaned softly, bringing her hands to his chest. He pulled the straps of her dress down and cupped her breasts. They were the perfect size, a generous handful. He played with her perky nipples while he nibbled on her neck. From the noises she was making, she was enjoying the attention. It gave him a little rush. His cock twitched.

His hand moved lower and found her soft wet folds, velvety, responsive. She whimpered and lifted her legs, planting those ridiculous heels on the edge of the desk. He looked down at the red marks his mouth had made on her neck; they made the tattoo stand out. His fingers teased her and his cock took some definite interest. *Again? Really?*

He moved back and dropped to his knees between her legs. She was pink, wet, swollen and floral. The sweet musk had an earthier base note he recognised as his own smell. He licked her, used his tongue to rummage on her clit. She jerked and cried out, thrusting her hips upwards. He grinned at her violent appreciation and renewed his assault.

~*~

Shelley moved her head onto his shoulder. They were laying on the couch in a sticky tangle of spent limbs. Their clothes, including her boots, were strewn around the room. The base was still thumping through the walls. 'What are you doing for Christmas?' she asked in a dreamy voice. After the tenth orgasm, she'd lost count and her body was in a sort of floating peace.

'Oh God, don't remind me,' he said.

'Why?'

'I haven't told my parents about Lindsay yet. My mother loves her. She will blame me for this.'

She wriggled around to look at him. 'Your mother will take her side over yours?'

He rested the back of his hand on his forehead and nodded, staring at the ceiling. 'She wants grandchildren.'

'Sounds like you got a lucky break, Rey. My parents tried to set me up with the guy of their choice. I escaped to the other side of the world to get away.'

'Ah! That explains the accent. You're English?'

She nodded. 'I have to go home for Christmas. I'm trying to decide whether to come back or not. They've offered an extension on my contract.'

'What do you want to do?'

'Not sure. I like it here. The weather is much better and I'm too far away for the parents to run my life for me. If I go home...' she trailed off.

'Running away from things doesn't resolve them you know.'

'Yeah, I know. But they wouldn't listen. I'm supposed to marry Phillip; our families have known each other forever. It's very medieval of them.'

'Well they can't force you to marry someone you don't want to.'

'No, but they can make my life hell for refusing to do what they want.'

'I hear you, Shelley.' He turned his head and smiled at her. He looked relaxed and happier than she had ever seen him, even before Lindsay. The two-faced bitch did the dirty on him. *What gives? He's a nice guy. Cuter than the average and way better than the average in the sack.*

'She didn't deserve you.'

'Hm.' Noncommittal. He shifted to lean on his elbow. 'I really don't want to talk about her. Tonight has been¬...' He hesitated as if looking for the right words. 'Incredible. You're different and this...' He touched her face, tracing a finger down her cheek to her neck where the tattoo was, the tattoo she got to symbolise breaking out of other people's webs. She would spin her own web, she had vowed, from that point forward. 'You've given me a different perspective,' he finished. Interesting that he seemed to get her so well, despite their outward differences.

On impulse she leaned in and said, 'How would you like a European Christmas?'

'What?'

'We could go skiing in Switzerland.'

He laughed. 'You're crazy, you know that?'

'Come on! Be crazy with me! You know you want to.'

'You're serious?' He shook his head. 'Christmas is less than a week away, how am I supposed to get a ticket? It'll cost a fortune.'

'Not an issue,' she waved a hand. She bit her lip and took a breath, time to tell him what no one else knew. 'My parents are loaded, if I tell them I want to bring a friend home for Christmas they'll pay for it.'

'You're joking.'

'No.'

He sat up and she watched his back trying to read what he was thinking from the set of his shoulders. Her heart was beating hard in her chest.

He swung his legs round so that he was sitting on the couch, then he hauled her up onto his lap. 'Thanks for the offer, but no.' She dropped her eyes, trying to mask her disappointment. She searched for something flippant to say, so he wouldn't see how much his rejection hurt. But he went on, 'If I come, I'll pay my own way.' He spoke over the top of her head.

'So you'll come?' She held her breath, unable to hide the excitement in her voice.

'I'll think about it.' His tone was cautious and yet, *he wanted to, didn't he?*

She grinned and kissed him. 'We'll have so much fun.' She paused a moment and then added, in case he was getting the wrong idea. 'Just fun. No commitments. Just fun, okay?'

Two weeks later

Their plane circled the Brisbane airport, with Shelley asleep on his shoulder. It had been a crazy week in London. They hadn't gone skiing in Switzerland, but he *had* met her parents and stayed in their three-storey London mansion. He'd also been introduced to Philip, who turned out to be a real live lord. Shelley's father was a viscount and her family a true British aristocracy. That was something he'd not seen coming. Shelley was full of surprises.

Shelley's rebellion was easy to understand, even if it was a bit extreme. And they'd had fun as she had promised. Sightseeing, social engagements. *Lots* of mind blowing sex.

He'd still had to deal with his parents. He'd given them the news by phone that he was going to the UK for Christmas and, by the way, he'd broken off his engagement to Lindsay. His mother, as predicted, wasn't happy.

She would be even less happy when he introduced Shelley as Lindsay's replacement. Not that he'd mention that to Shelley yet. She was still firmly in 'friends with benefits' mode.

But he knew what he wanted, and it was Shelley Carlisle. Spider web tattoo and all.

Lover's Moon
By
Caitlyn Lynch

'Kneel, Gryllus son of Gallyn!' the High Priestess intoned and Gryllus slid to his knees there on the tournament ground, blood running from several minor wounds and turning the sands around him red.

'You have done well this day,' the priestess told him, leaning forward to place the huge *labrys* she carried before him. Intricate engravings covered the golden blades of the double-headed ceremonial axe; Gryllus found himself studying them in fascination.

'Take him and bind his wounds,' the priestess instructed her acolytes. 'Seven nights hence, at the full moon, he must begin his duties.'

Gryllus' hand curled around the carved wooden handle of the *labrys* as gentle hands pulled at him, urging him to his feet. As he stumbled towards the temple, guided by the priestesses surrounding him, the aging warrior he had just defeated wept in the dust, the vibrant tattoos which had covered his heavily muscled arms and chest slowly fading away.

Gryllus had never received such pampering in his life. He was bathed in scented waters, his wounds tenderly bandaged, and food and wine were served to him by priestesses who would no longer look him in the eye.

Without being falsely vain, he knew that women found him attractive. Tall, well-muscled and black-haired, his face unscarred, his eyes an unusual light golden colour, he had never lacked for bedmates. Blood still boiling after the fight, he reached out and caught the arm of Aithra, a pretty young woman whose blankets he had shared many times before, pulling her into his lap.

'Will you not share this victory with me, my sweet?'

He hardly expected her terrified screams, her desperate struggles to escape. Startled, he let her go at once and she scrambled away from him on hands and knees, babbling, 'I didn't mean to, I'm sorry!' as the High Priestess frowned down at her.

'Selene is a jealous Goddess,' the High Priestess said disapprovingly. 'Hurry away, Aithra, and mind that you never touch the Guardian again.' She waved away the other priestesses, who had drawn back from Gryllus as far as the room would allow, and they fled in Aithra's wake.

'What in Hades...?' Gryllus gazed after the fleeing women in shock.

The High Priestess knelt before him. 'You do not yet understand, and I am forbidden from explaining to you,' she said, her dark brown eyes holding his unwaveringly. 'But the Guardian must know no mortal woman.'

By '*know*' she meant '*bed,*' Gryllus correctly interpreted and made a disgusted face. '*That* was never mentioned when we were told that becoming the Guardian was the highest honour a warrior might achieve!'

'There are many things that are not told to you until you step into the inner sanctum,' the priestess replied. 'But know this, Gryllus. Aithra will be spared because I could see clearly that she did not seek to tempt you. But next time you seek intimacy with a mortal woman, it will mean her death.'

Furious as the priestess departed, leaving him alone, Gryllus threw himself down on the cushions that padded his new bed.

'I never signed on for celibacy,' he muttered, glaring at the mosaic of the crescent moon shining over the sea that covered one wall of the chamber. Reaching down, he lifted the short *chiton* that barely covered his groin, wrapped his hand around his own cock. 'Well, at least she never said anything about not seeking my own relief!'

~ * ~

The morning brought three of the oldest priestesses to him; they checked his wounds and bandaged them afresh, provided bread and meat to break his fast.

'I'd like to speak to Ionus,' Gryllus named the opponent he had vanquished the previous day. Ionus had been Guardian for seventeen years, not much less time than Gryllus had been alive. Surely the former Guardian could tell him some of what to expect.

'Ionus's time has passed,' he was told.

'I'd still like to speak to him,' he pressed.

'It is cruel to ask him to look upon his successor, the man who has earned what he may never have again!' Heads shook disapprovingly and they departed, leaving him alone again and more puzzled than ever.

~ * ~

By the fifth day of being sequestered in the temple, Gryllus grew impatient at his forced inactivity. Examining his wounds, the High Priestess declared that he was healed enough for his marking to begin and the priestesses brought in the equipment.

He had known this was coming—but warriors who aspired to one day become Guardian were required to keep their skin clean, so he wasn't at all prepared for how much it would hurt. They began with a golden crescent moon over his heart, and by the time that was done he had asked for a piece of wood to clench between his teeth, to keep himself from crying out.

For a full day and a night and into the next day the priestesses worked his skin with their needles and inks, covering his chest, arms and shoulders with designs and symbols, dedicating his flesh to their Goddess. At long last they declared themselves satisfied, spreading healing unguents over his skin that did little to suppress the burning, stinging agony.

'Drink this,' the High Priestess said gently, taking the piece of wood from between his teeth and offering a goblet of wine in its place. 'Sleep now, Gryllus. Tonight you go to the Goddess.'

There must have been something more than wine in the cup, for his eyes closed after a few mouthfuls despite his pain.

109

~ * ~

When he woke, the sun was setting. It took him a little while to realise that his skin no longer stung so much as it had. Standing, he moved his arms experimentally, shaking his head with surprise as his skin shifted over his muscles without the sharp agony he had expected. There was little sensation now beyond a dull throb that he could ignore. Taking up the ceremonial *labrys* axe, he left his chamber and walked deeper into the labyrinthine temple, through halls he had walked since he was a child.

Coming to the closed doors of the inner sanctum, he found the High Priestess awaiting him. She studied him in silence, examining his tattoos, the simple cloth wrapped around his waist the only thing that kept him from being quite naked.

Turning, she opened the massive timber double doors and gestured him to follow her. Gryllus followed, wondering what he would see; it was death for any but the Guardian or the High Priestess to enter the inner sanctum of Selene's temple.

He hadn't expected a large, stone-walled room with no ceiling, though, thinking about it, a sanctum where the moonlight could not enter would make no sense in a temple dedicated to the moon goddess. The only thing in the room was a large, comfortable-looking bed, mounded with pillows. Staring at it, Gryllus frowned in utter confusion. He was expected to *sleep* here? That did not seem like an appropriate way to revere his Goddess.

Turning to the High Priestess, he asked, 'What is this? I do not understand.'

She smiled, mysterious in the fading light. 'You will. When I am gone, use the *labrys* to bar the door.'

That did not seem like an appropriate thing to do with the ceremonial weapon, either. 'Wait! What must I do then?' he cried, but she was already leaving, pulling the great doors closed behind her.

Cursing under his breath before feeling ashamed for doing so in his Goddess' temple, Gryllus supposed the only thing to do was obey what he had been told. The light was fading fast and he could barely see. Swiftly he pushed the *labrys'* carved wooden handle into the metal hasps affixed to the rear side of the doors, bolting them closed.

Turning, he peered around the room. The sky had darkened to a deep blue, the stars beginning to twinkle, but he could see little. The moon would rise soon; he supposed when that happened he should pray to Selene for guidance. Angry and frustrated, wishing that he had been told more of what he must do, he paced out the sanctum's walls, trying to discover if there was any other clue inside the room as to what his duties might entail.

Slowly, Gryllus realised that he could see better. Not merely because his eyes were adapting to the lack of light, but because there *was* more light. The source of it was indistinct and he looked around in confusion before realising that *he* was the source. More specifically, his tattoos.

Red, green and blue glowed faintly from the inks beneath his skin, the golden crescent moon over his heart glowing brighter yet. They no longer pained him at all, Gryllus realised, gazing down at himself in wonder.

'Ionus,' a voice called and his head snapped up, eyes widening, for he had barred the door. Nobody should be inside the sanctum but himself, and yet on the other side of the roofless chamber, where a beam of moonlight angled in to strike the wall, there stood a woman.

Tall and dark-haired, with skin paler than anyone Gryllus had ever seen, she wore a long white gown, pinned at one shoulder with a silver brooch. Crowned by a silver diadem shaped like the crescent moon, her glossy midnight-black hair fell to her ankles, swirling around her as she took a step towards him.

'You are not Ionus.'

Her voice was high and sweet, like the sound of a flute playing, the most beautiful voice that Gryllus had ever heard, just as she was undoubtedly the most beautiful woman he had ever seen. Sudden understanding struck him. He slid to his knees and bent forward to press his brow to the cold stone floor, terrified to look upon a deity lest he be struck down for such blasphemy.

'My Goddess,' he choked out.

Selene laughed, softly musical, and paced forward, her gown and her hair swishing about her slender legs as she moved, walking all the way around him. 'No, indeed, you are not Ionus, my young warrior.' A finger brushed lightly over his back, tracing the image which spread from shoulder to shoulder, her silver moon chariot drawn by two winged white steeds. 'Tell me your name.'

'Gryllus son of Gallyn.' He could barely get the words out. Her touch felt like cold fire crawling across his skin. Beneath the wrap around his waist, his cock leaped to attention. Silently cursing his wayward body, he tried to will his arousal away. Surely thoughts such as those which had raced through his mind upon first seeing her beauty were blasphemous!

'Gryllus,' she said the name slowly, as though tasting it, savouring it. He had to suppress a groan as the single word seemed to reverberate through him. Names had great power in the mouth of a goddess. 'My Guardian. Rise, and look upon me.'

He was powerless to resist the command in her voice. Standing, he slowly lifted his eyes to her face; he was tall, but she looked him in the eye, easily the tallest woman he had ever seen.

She is no mere woman, he reminded himself firmly. *She is divine, a goddess.* He only wished that his body would listen—and prayed that she would not look down to see his arousal pushing hard against the thin cloth.

Stars burned in her eyes. Awed, he gazed upon her with open reverence, until she smiled and reached out to lay her hand over the crescent moon tattooed on his chest.

From her hand over his heart a soft light began to spread through her skin, turning its pale beauty luminescent, glowing like the moon itself.

'We are given strength by the worship of our followers,' Selene told him. 'You, my Guardian, are the avatar for that devotion. By your touch, my divinity is assured.'

He finally understood. The tattoos were somehow the method of storing power raised by the prayers of her followers, and he was merely the vessel to deliver it to her. Honoured, he bowed his head.

'All that I am is yours to command, my Goddess.'

'Good.' She smiled, a quicksilver flash of white teeth under lips as red as blood. 'Because the night is young, and I have been too long unsatisfied.' Taking her hand from his chest, she brought it to her shoulder, unclasped the brooch there, and let her gown fall to the floor.

Gryllus's mouth fell open. He took a step back, wide-eyed and suddenly fearful again. Surely to look upon her naked form would mean his death; no mortal should look upon such divine beauty!

Selene moved right along with him, her fingers hooking into the cloth folded at his waist, sweeping it away to leave him just as naked as she. Her tongue slipped out to wet her red lips at the sight of his erect cock.

'Oh, you are a very fine Guardian, indeed.' Turning away, she walked over to the bed, lay down upon its plush surface, and opened her arms to him. 'Come to me, Gryllus.'

There was no command in her voice now. He could have resisted her order if he wished to, but what man would refuse *her*? He had already sworn himself to her service long before this night, besides. His feet moved before he had even made a conscious decision, carrying him to stand beside the bed. Selene reached out and took his hand, bringing it to her lips as her starry eyes gazed up at him.

'Show me your devotion, my Guardian,' she said, before pressing a kiss against his fingertips and drawing his hand down, trailing down the long elegant line of her slender throat, across her chest before placing it upon one of her high, rounded breasts.

Her meaning was unmistakable, just as her beauty was incomparable. Doubts receded, swamped by rising lust; after all, Gryllus thought, Ionus had served as the Guardian for seventeen years. If he was required to serve Selene in bed as part of his duties, well, that was no hardship at all. Kneeling beside her on the bed, he leaned down to kiss her lips.

Slender arms wound around his neck and pulled with incredible strength, dragging him down atop her, their bodies pressed together all along their length. Selene's long legs twined around his hips and she pushed up against him, rubbing her cleft along the length of his cock. He groaned into her mouth as he discovered that she was already wet, silky juices coating his arousal.

'You are eager, my warrior.' Selene laughed as he lifted his head, gasping for breath.

'You are a goddess, divine in your beauty. How could I not be eager?' Still, he would not have her be disappointed in him.

Her smile told him that he had found words that pleased her, at least. Determined to worship every part of her, he set his lips to the luminous pale skin of her throat, kissing and licking gently at tender flesh, working his way down to the perfect globes of her breasts.

When he took her nipple into his mouth and suckled, Selene sighed with pleasure, running her fingers into his hair to hold him close to her breast.

'Ah, a man who knows how to pleasure a woman. I will not have to teach you everything, I see.'

Gryllus lifted his head and gave her a curious look. She chuckled. 'My last Guardian was a devout man... a little *too* devout. He swore celibacy before he even came to manhood. I'm afraid I came as rather a shock to him.'

He had to laugh at the thought of how he would have reacted to her if he'd been innocent of the pleasures of the flesh. Sliding lower, he said in between kisses pressed to the soft skin of her belly, 'I hope you will not find me ignorant, my goddess.'

Selene smiled with satisfaction as he nuzzled the silky triangle of black hair between her legs before moving lower still, tongue stroking over her folds, parting them to caress the sensitive nub of her clitoris.

She was wet already, and growing more so under his ministrations. Gryllus had always liked bringing a woman to pleasure with his tongue, and for all her divinity it seemed Selene enjoyed it as much as any mortal woman, though she tasted sweeter. Sweet as ambrosia itself, he fancied, nectar of the gods. He buried his face and lapped greedily, listening to her passionate cries increase in volume until she shuddered, her thighs clenching briefly against his shoulders, and let out a long, high wail of ecstasy.

Gryllus fully expected her to lie back against the pillows, briefly spent. He was not at all prepared for her to rear up off the bed, grasp him by his shoulders and flip him to his back as easily as he would handle a lamb, before climbing atop him to straddle his hips.

Wide-eyed, he stared up at her, and Selene chuckled. 'Does my strength surprise you, Gryllus?'

'Yes,' he admitted, guessing that she would sense a lie in an instant. 'I have fought against female warriors of renown; their skill was great, but their strength could never match that of a man. Your strength is far beyond mine, and that should not be possible.'

'Never forget that I am not mortal,' she told him. 'I am a goddess, *your* goddess—and you are mine now, my mortal beloved. While we may only be together within these walls, I will not share you with any other.'

Selene is a jealous goddess, he remembered the High Priestess telling Aithra. Gazing up at Selene, at the luminous glory of her skin, her starry eyes, the magnificent cape of her midnight hair falling around her body, Gryllus shook his head.

'No other could compare to you,' he told her truthfully.

Selene smiled, her hands trailing lightly over the still-glowing tattoos on his chest before they slid lower to firmly clasp his cock.

Gryllus hadn't thought that he could get any harder, but as Selene's slender hands wrapped around him, another rush of blood engorged his arousal still further, making him swell thicker and longer than he had ever been.

'Oh, Goddess,' he whimpered, hands clawing at the sheets beneath him.

'I am here, my Guardian,' she said on a soft laugh, before raising herself up and lowering down onto him.

He had to throw his head back and clench his teeth, because she felt beyond amazing, the hot wet grasp of her tight tunnel sheathing him almost more than he could bear. Spurting his load now like a green lad would displease Selene, he was quite sure, and that was the very last thing he wished for. He had won the right to be her Guardian, the avatar of her worshippers' devotion, but to be her lover as well was a privilege far above that.

Selene sighed as she sank down, taking him to the hilt with one slow roll of her hips. A smile curved her perfect red lips;

she reached down and traced the defined muscles of his chest with one sharp, black-tinted fingernail. 'Gryllus,' she sighed his name, and he moaned as the power of it reverberated through his whole body.

She felt so light sitting astride him, ethereal, as though she was barely there at all. He brought his hands to her hips hesitantly, afraid to grip too hard, at least until she laughed and told him to hang on tight.

'Else I might fall off!'

He thought she spoke in jest, but the first powerful roll of her hips caught him by surprise, and he tightened his grasp instinctively.

'Good,' Selene said. 'That's it...' And suddenly she was riding him at a gallop, thigh muscles stronger than any human's could ever be, flexing to lift her up and down along his aching, throbbing shaft.

'Goddess!' he cried out instinctively, clinging to her tightly. She laughed and went faster, faster, until the friction and pleasure were too much for him to bear.

~ * ~

Gryllus roared his ecstasy to the night sky; writhing atop him as his seed pumped hotly deep within her, Selene reached her own peak with a joyous shriek.

'Oh, my warrior,' she crooned, laying down atop his heaving chest, moaning with renewed pleasure as more power surged into her from his still-charged tattoos. Soon the power stored within them would be drained entirely, refilling again over the coming day as her worshippers offered up prayers. Right now, though, the goddess of the moon revelled in the sensation, a heady rush atop the lingering pleasure or her climax.

Gryllus's hand came up, hesitantly stroking her silken hair. She arched into his touch with a soft hum. He was gazing at her with pure reverence in his expression, and she realised suddenly that the power surging into her through his tattoos was not being gathered from her worshippers. It was *his* devotion, and his alone.

Selene had been adored by her Guardians before, had been worshipped as the divine being she was. Still, she had never been the complete centre of anyone's world before, both sun and moon to them, as she saw herself reflected now in the dark eyes of the young warrior beneath her.

Gently, almost wonderingly, she touched his face, caressing the strong line of his jaw, exploring the texture of his short beard. He turned his head to press a kiss to her fingertips, and Selene did something that she had never done before, in the many long centuries since she had first discovered how to harvest power from her devotees through her Guardian.

She gave some of her power *back*.

Gryllus gasped, his eyes going wide as strength suddenly flooded into his tired body. His flagging cock stiffened, a surge of energy racing through his blood making him feel strong enough to wrestle Ares himself and win.

Selene smiled.

Flexing powerful muscles, Gryllus rolled them until Selene lay beneath him, her midnight hair spreading over the white sheets, no paler than her softly luminous skin.

'Tell me that you can stay a while longer,' he begged, his hips shifting to begin the sensual dance between them again.

'Until the last beams of moonlight leave this room, my warrior,' she told him. 'And then I must leave you.'

'No time to waste, then,' Gryllus said with a smile, and she threw back her head and laughed for joy.

~ * ~

Gryllus was only vaguely aware of Selene rising from the bed as the moonlight began to fade, going to the door to unbar it. She returned to his side and stroked a gentle hand down his flank before bending to kiss his damp brow tenderly.

'Sleep, my warrior,' she whispered. 'I will come to you when the moon rises once again.'

He couldn't even muster the energy for a grunt in response. Though he wanted to watch her go, see if she really did ride up into the night sky in a silver chariot drawn by winged white horses, his eyelids were too heavy to hold open.

His last thought was that he now understood just why Ionus had fought as though possessed by demons of the Underworld for the right to remain Selene's Guardian. Seventeen years was far too short a time to be blessed by her divine love.

Serendipity
By
Dina Bridges

'Your 1pm has arrived, Seren. I'll show them in.'

Her PA turned to walk away, but Seren stopped her.

'Tara, before you go, remind me again of their names, would you please?'

'Sure. Laura and Michelle,' she said, and closed the door behind her. Seren reached into her desk drawer and pulled out two business cards.

Seren Silver
Head of Marketing
Dubrille & Co.

The title still made her smile, two years on from achieving it. And why not? Being the youngest woman to join the board of directors at London's most revered marketing agency was something she'd worked hard to achieve. She had every right to be proud.

But it hadn't come without sacrifice. She couldn't remember the last time she'd had a man in her life. Not that there had been a lack of offers, but by the time she'd put in the hours needed to shine in this cutthroat industry, she was far too exhausted to give sex a second thought.

She stood and ran her hands down her cream-coloured cotton blouse to smooth out the creases.

This sex drought is starting to take its toll, she realised, as her nipples stood to attention in response to her touch.

There was a knock on the door and Tara walked back in, accompanied with a man and a woman. *Hmm. Does the tall guy with the dark curls go by the name of Laura or Michelle?*

'—and this is Michel Lasson'

Seren didn't hear Tara's other words, they didn't seem to matter.

Her hand belied the chaos in her brain and went out automatically for a formal handshake. There was no mistaking it; those unusual but striking features belonged to *her* Michel. Straight, narrow nose: tick. Almond-shaped, chocolate-coloured eyes, tick. Angular jaw, tick. Sensual stare that turned her insides to mush, double tick. Other than a single streak of grey in his dark brown curls and new crinkles at the corners of his eyes, he looked just the same as the last time she'd seen him ten years earlier.

She could never forget him. How could she when he was imprinted on her brain. Her heart. Her *body*.

Her thought went to the indelible ink that flowed across her ribcage. Did he still have his? Did he still bear that word across his torso that was meant to lock them together forever? Did his thoughts fly across the Channel every time the black lettering stared back at his reflection? Or had he had it removed? If you take away the ink does it take away the memory? She doubted it, or she would have done it long ago.

'Seren, you work here now?'

The way he said her name, with his rolled French 'r's still made her abdomen tighten.

With the shock of seeing him again rippling through her body, all she could do was nod silently and paste a banal smile on her face that made her cheek muscles ache.

'Felicitations, you made Marketing Director. Your dream came true,' he said.

He still had hold of her hand, not having let it go since she offered it him to shake. A shadow of sadness flickered across his face as he congratulated her. Her heart leapt out to him, but only for a moment, until she reminded herself that leaving had been his doing, not hers.

She managed to compose herself and switch the conversation to business. Avoiding eye contact helped her stay on track, but every so often she gave in to the pull of those magnetic pupils of his. His gaze locked her in and she stuttered on her words. The red-hot memories came flooding back: his large hands cupping her buttocks, pulling her territorially onto his toned, naked body; his mouth latching onto her nipple as the roughness of his tongue made her groan with longing; his smooth shaft, standing hard and proud, ripe for love-making.

~ * ~

He didn't have to be a mind reader to know what she was thinking. Her body was giving her away. Thankfully his assistant, Laura, had her head fixed on her notepad as she documented their conversation fastidiously. He posed a complex question, ensuring she had plenty to write down, while he allowed his gaze to drift to where Seren's nipples were pushing through her bra.

Her breasts looked fantastic, even if they were encased in a stiff, formal blouse. The last time he'd felt them, soft and plump beneath his palms, they'd been smaller. Still beautiful but not as rounded and full as they were now. Now in her thirties, Seren was even more of a turn-on than she had been at twenty-one. Curvier, more womanly. Fleshier and peachy, she looked like a fertile goddess whose figure was worthy of worship.

The sight of her, combined with the memories of all those years ago, caused his groin to ache. He almost sighed with relief when his assistant excused herself for a comfort break.

'More coffee, Michel?'

Seren's offer came several seconds after Laura had left the room and was an obvious and awkward attempt to sever the chemistry between them. He didn't answer, but she walked around to his side of the desk anyway to retrieve his empty cup. In one smooth motion, he caught her wrist, stood up and pushed her back against the table until the edge dug into her thighs. She opened her mouth to object but he beat her to it.

'This is crazy, Seren. We can't carry on like this, trying to get through this ridiculous meeting when all we want to do is make love to one another.'

'Speak for yourself,' she said, her blue eyes flashing with indignation.

'I *am*. You're driving me wild here, Seren, and I want you. God, I want you.'

'It's not exactly the time or the place, Michel. And we hardly parted on the best terms!'

She wished her words could quell her own libido but they didn't. Her swollen breasts pressed against his firm chest, begging to be stimulated.

'Your mouth says one thing, *mon amour*, but your body says another. Tell me you don't want to feel me inside you ever again and, I promise, I'll leave you alone.'

'I…' She tried to object but the feel of his hardened cock, pressing against her stomach so invitingly, caused her voice to taper to a whisper. Damn him for being right. She *did* want to feel him again, to sense the weight of his body on hers as he rode them both into a sexual utopia, just like he used to do, night after night for three wonderful years of their lives.

That Seren, flirty, fun and care-free Seren, who made love to the man she believed she was going to spend the rest of her life with, seemed like a distant memory. A world away. She wanted to be *that* Seren again, even if it was just for one night.

He traced a finger down the side of her face and she closed her eyes, savouring the sensation.

She didn't allow her eyes to open even when she felt his deliciously hungry mouth crushing against hers. She parted her lips to let his tongue enter, and tangled hers together with his, colliding and clashing against each other, their saliva as hot as molten lava.

His mouth still upon hers, he pushed a hand up her shirt. He reached inside one of her bra cups and gently squeezed. His touch was like therapy. She swallowed a moan, trying to keep her pleasure to herself, a challenge which became all the harder when he began rolling her tightened nipple between his thumb and forefinger.

'I need you, Seren,' he whispered between kisses. 'These ten years have been torture without you.'

His hand left her breast and travelled down to the hem of her pencil skirt. She grasped the edge of the desk and tipped her head back. His lips found her neck, and covered every inch of it in light, feathery kisses.

'Michel, stop. Laura will be back any minute.' Seren heard herself saying the words but hoped he wouldn't heed her warning. She couldn't bear for him to stop, not now.

He didn't. Instead, he walked the pads of his fingers up her bare inner thigh. She inhaled sharply, waiting for the much-needed friction of his touch at her core. She held her breath and waited, aware of the trickle between her legs—a slick of cream which coated her sex and soaked into her underwear.

The touch came and her sexual reflex kicked in. Perching her bottom onto the edge of the desk she opened her legs as wide as her skirt allowed.

'Jesus, Seren,' Michel said, feeling how wet she was for him. The arousal in his voice turned her on even more, and she pushed her hips forward to gain more pressure from his finger. She froze. A click clack of heels was coming down the corridor. Shit, Laura! She shoved his arm away from her, jumped off the desk and smoothed her skirt, just as the door opened.

'Laura, I was just getting more coffees. Can I offer you one?' She could tell by the brunette's confused expression that they looked guilty. Or at least Seren did. A sideways glance at Michel told her that he didn't look remotely ruffled. His body language exuded coolness, and he ran a hand casually through his curls. The hand that had just been stroking the most intimate part of her.

Seren walked back to her chair and sat down. The wetness between her legs had cooled, leaving her uncomfortable and unsatisfied throughout the rest of the meeting.

An hour later and it was time for goodbye handshakes. No offers of dinner, no promises of follow up meetings, just a transactional farewell. And then he was gone. Like any other client from any other company. But this wasn't just another client. This was Michel Lasson; the man she'd lost her virginity to, the man she'd agreed to marry, the man who had broken her heart. And now he was gone. Again.

~ * ~

It was 10pm and Seren lay in bed, alone, awake. Her body still smouldered from his touch. She thumped the pillow in a bid to rid herself of her sexual—and mental—frustration. It didn't work.

Seeing Michel again had stirred up old memories she thought she'd left in the past. She ran her palm down her naked body to where the needle had penetrated her skin all those years before.

She'd kept the tattoo. Although she barely admitted it to herself, she'd kept it because having it removed would break the magic of its sentiment. Just like tattoos were forever, so was their love. That had been the plan anyway. How naive they'd been! Holding each other's hand as the tattooist's drill pierced their young skin, they'd had their love marked permanently on each other's bodies.

She felt a prickle between her legs as her body responded to the touch of her hand on her ribcage. She moved her hand from her torso to her pubic bone and began to stroke the downy hair. She used the other hand to squeeze her breast, and her nipple hardened between her fingers in response. Her heartbeat quickened and her need to seek release grew. Lowering her hand, she started to massage the sensitive dome at the centre of her core. As the wetness intensified, her fingers slicked over the contours of her body. She increased the pressure and let her memories take over

She lay on his chest and tipped her head up to look up at him. He grinned down at her with that gorgeous, wide smile of his and scooped her up so their mouths met. His kiss took her breath away, his fingers tangled in her hair...

Blood flowed to her core and she let the pads of her fingers explore the inside of her sex, the part that had not been touched for so long.

They were one now. She was straddling him, grinding against him as he guided her hips up and down his hardened shaft. He filled her body with his. The smooth ridges of his member glided into her. She splayed her hands over his chest, over his pounding heart. Their breathing quickened in unison as climax approached.

She flipped over onto her front and brought her tingling, wet pussy in contact with the bed sheet. She rotated her hips forward to achieve maximum pressure and drove herself up and down, desperately chasing release.

His eyes never left hers as he climbed closer and closer to orgasm. He

groaned out her name, followed by a string of French as he came. Holding
her hips in place he pulsed his seed into her. Seeing the pleasure her body
had brought him drove her over the edge and seconds later she was right
there with him in ecstasy. Gripping her waist, he waited for her waves of
pleasure to subside before grinning and pulling her back on top of him for
an embrace from which she never wanted to be freed.

Seconds before orgasm engulfed her she stopped and let the
sensation go. How did she think pleasuring herself alone like
this was going to make her feel better when, tonight, somewhere
in the same city for the first time in ten years, lay Michel?

~ * ~

'Seren. What are you doing here?'

She took advantage of him opening the door wide when
she'd knocked and walked into his hotel room without waiting
for an invitation. It hadn't been difficult to work out where he'd
be staying, not when the hotel where they'd first consummated
their love was minutes from her office.

'Perhaps it's fate.' She spat the word at him, laying on the
sarcasm. 'You always were convinced we were destined for one
another, weren't you, Michel? But that theory hasn't worked too
well for us so far, has it?' The thought of his words as he'd left
her that day, ten years ago, were branded onto her brain: *If it's*
meant to be, mon amour, we'll meet again.

She snapped back into the present and realised she was
crying, just as she'd done the last time she'd seen him, when
he'd walked out on her.

'Why did you do it, Michel? Why did you leave? Don't you
know how much I loved you?' She swiped the tears furiously
from her cheeks, hating herself for her display of emotion.

He came over to her and pulled her close into his chest. She
could smell him—remnants of the day's cologne with a
generous drenching of testosterone. It had been so long since
she'd had his beautiful, erotic scent in her nostrils and it brought
with it a rush of bittersweet memories.

'Seren.'

The way he said her name, so full of love and tenderness,
made her sob harder. The pain she had been denying, the pain
she had suppressed by pretending it didn't matter because her

career was more important, all came flooding into her heart as if she was experiencing it for the first time.

She didn't know how long she cried or how long he held her but when the tears finally stopped flowing she felt like a ten year weight had been lifted.

'You broke my heart you know, the day you walked away,' she said.

'You broke mine.'

She pulled away from his chest and looked up at him.

'But it was your choice to leave. You were the one who ended things and went back to France. Why would you do that if you were hurting too?'

He sighed and lowered his head. A single dark curl flopped over one eye. She wanted to stroke the hair back and kiss him over and over, telling him it didn't matter now that they'd found each other again. But she couldn't. While she retained a modicum of self-worth she needed to hear it from him.

'We were always the right ones for each other, Seren, we just met at the wrong time. Things were fantastic while we were studying but once you got a job, you became a different person. You were only interested in achieving great things at work. And why shouldn't you? You'd worked so hard, you deserved it. But our relationship suffered, and my young ego couldn't cope with it. I had to leave, to give you space to live *your* life.'

'Why, Michel? We could have talked about it, got through. But you didn't even try, you just came home one night, packed your bags, kissed me on the cheek and declared us over.'

'No. I said over *for now*.'

'You said if it was meant to be we'd meet again, but we didn't, did we? Not till now. How could *that* be my destiny? A decade of trying to convince myself I didn't care about you because my career was all that mattered. I've been lying to myself for a third of my life, and all because you were happy to leave things to fate!'

His eyes narrowed and his expression darkened.

'Take off your dress, Seren.'

His voice had changed from a gentle tone to commanding, so commanding she didn't think to argue. She reached to pull down her zip, wiggled out of her dress and let it fall to the floor in a puddle of cotton. Never breaking contact with her eyes, he slowly undid his shirt, button by button, cufflink by cufflink, until it gaped open to show a strip of his light olive skin and a spattering of dark hair across his broad chest. She didn't wait for him to do the rest. She pushed the shirt off his shoulders to the floor, leaving his athletic upper body completely exposed.

Jet black letters snaked across his side. He'd kept it. She smiled, and he reached out to stroke the skin where the tattoo wound around her own torso.

He drew his arms around her back, unclipped her bra and flung it to the floor as if annoyed with it for getting in his way. His breathing was heavier, more ragged and he searched her eyes as if looking for answers.

'I can't tell you how much I've missed you,' he said. Without giving her chance to respond he pulled her against him and kissed her as if his life depended on it.

'Look,' he said, when he finally wrenched his lips from hers. She followed his gaze to the full-length mirror across the room. With their bodies pressed together their tattoos joined up and spelled the word they had let seal their fate.

'Serendipity,' she read out loud.

'A chance encounter meant to be,' he said. 'We met by pure chance yet are meant to be together.'

'At least you got *Seren*,' she laughed, 'I got *dipity*. It doesn't even make sense on its own!'

'It makes sense when you're next to me,' he said, without a trace of mirth. 'Which is exactly where you belong.'

She looked into his eyes, and saw them twinkling with love and desire.

'We were meant for each other, Seren,' he said.

She swallowed hard and wanted to tell him how she felt, but the emotions running through her were so strong she was worried if she tried to speak she might cry again.

~ * ~

He rested his big hands protectively on her bare shoulders and guided her towards the bed. When she couldn't go any further without falling onto it he stopped her and stroked his hands down her body until he met the top of her thong. Grasping the flimsy lace, he rolled it down to her thighs and let it slip to her ankles.

She looked so beautiful and vulnerable standing naked before him that the sight of her sent a pure, primitive desire pulsing through him.

He stroked his hands back up her body, placing one behind her head and the other in the smooth arch of her back. Gently, as if she were made of china, he lowered her to the bed. He ran his tongue from her neck, down to her naval and beyond.

Her moan turned him on more than he could think possible. On hearing it, he sank down to his knees and eased her thighs apart. He brought his lips to within centimetres of her most intimate area and paused to savour the sight and smell of her. Her slick folds glistened and her musky scent excited him as he breathed her in. He forced himself to hold back as he exhaled deeply, allowing the air to tickle the sensitive bundle of nerve endings which protruded enticingly at her centre.

She wriggled wantonly and murmured pleas for him to replace his breath with his touch. He kept the tease for as long as he could, until the wait was torturous for them both. Finally, when he could stand the anticipation no more, he began to lap at her, licking every millimetre of her sex except for the nub in the middle.

She writhed, attempting to deepen the stimulation, arching her back to push her body harder against his mouth, trying to catch her clit against the roughness of his tongue. But he deliberately avoided the hardened mound, making her wait for the friction she craved.

He took his time to appreciate the hot, wet taste of pure woman, of Seren. How he'd missed touching her, kissing her, *tasting* her. Unable to hold himself back any longer he ran his tongue slowly over her womanly opening, feasting on her delicious juices as he did so, all the way up to where her clitoris was desperately awaiting some overdue attention.

She gasped as he teasingly circled it, and begged him to sate her. He obeyed, flicking his tongue over its surface. Her sweet little nook was so swollen with arousal it had grown rock hard. The feel of it on his lips drove him wild. Unable to stop himself, he sank his mouth on top it, sucking and licking in a frenzy of carnal desire.

She screamed out in pleasure and reached her hands to grab the back of his head. She clutched at his hair to hold him in place and opened her legs even wider to give him full access. He squeezed his eyes shut against the sharpness of his hair being pulled, enjoying the heady combination of pleasure mingled with pain.

She climaxed and her womanly crest pulsated against his tongue. The urgency in his groin to be inside her reached crisis point. His erection throbbed, demanding to enter her.

Although it was almost the undoing of him, he waited patiently for her breathing to return to normal, then lay back on the bed and pulled her on top of him so that her breasts were above his face. Her hardened nipples pointed at him, inviting his mouth to close around them. He latched on to them, suckling the knotted pink peaks, as if drawing vital sustenance.

His mouth was still on her breast when he felt her hand reach down between his legs and wrap around the part of him which cried out for her the most. She pulled away from him to sit up, and for a moment he longed to have her nipple back in his mouth. But then realising her need was just as great as his, he drank in the glorious sight of her.

Still clenching his cock, she positioned herself over him and guided him inside her. She was tight, hot, and wet. Just as she had been the very first time. He entered her slowly at first, allowing her to become accustomed to his size before pushing further, deeper and harder.

Watching her wriggle on top of him, pressing herself against his pelvis as he thrust inside her, was the most erotic thing he'd ever seen. He didn't care that the groan accompanying his orgasm was so doused in masculinity that it came out more like an animalistic roar. He only cared that he was back in bed with the woman he loved. The only woman he'd *ever* loved.

~ * ~

The morning light streamed in from the window. Seren lay on her side, awake, as Michel's body spooned hers. She listened to his deep, rhythmic breathing as he slept and for the first time in a long time she felt she was finally in the right place. In bed, in the arms of the man who treasured her and, as he'd told her in their post coital heart to heart, who had never stopped loving her.

'Why didn't you come and find me? It wouldn't have been that hard,' she'd asked him. He explained they'd both needed time apart, to achieve their own goals, before finding each other again.

'We were lucky we met, but unlucky it had been too soon,' he'd said.

She thought back to their conversation and smiled.

'So, you making a meeting in my office today was planned? You knew I'd be there? It wasn't serendipity at all?'

He smiled back and made his confession. *'I loved you too much to leave things to fate. I couldn't live without you a day longer, I had to come and see you. If you'd have turned me down it would have broken me all over again, but waiting any more wasn't an option.'*

Michel's strong arm rested heavily over her body in a protective embrace, over her half of their matching tattoo. She laughed to herself, quietly, so as not to wake him. Ha, serendipity indeed! She stroked the hair on his arm from his elbow to his wrist and brought his hand up to rest his hot palm on her chest. Her naked breast felt sensitive under his touch. She put it down to their frantic lovemaking sessions, which had become more and more heated as the night had progressed.

Michel began to stir and moaned his appreciation as he realised he was waking to a generous handful of Seren's breast. Her nipple tightened in response and he massaged the hardened peak with his index finger.

'Good morning,' she said, her voice husky from their night together.

'Morning, *mon amour,*' he said, rolling her over onto her back and nuzzling her neck. 'I'd give anything right now to make love to you, but it would make you late for work.'

'Oh, I wouldn't worry about that,' she said, twirling one of his dark curls around her finger. 'I've already decided to pull a sicky, so you can ravish my body all day if you want to.'

He propped himself up on his elbows and looked at her with raised eyebrows.

'You? Phone in sick? When was the last time you did that?'

She laughed. 'Never! Even when I've been genuinely sick. But that's the old me. Workaholic Seren is no more. I've waited ten years for you to come back and work can take a back seat for once.'

He regarded her in silence for several seconds before speaking. 'Seren, marry me.'

Her heart leapt in her chest and she thought she would burst with happiness. She fought hard to keep a straight face.

'Well, that depends,' she said.

He furrowed his brow. 'What on?'

'On what you intend to do with this.' She reached under the sheet and closed her hand around his erection.

Realising what she meant, he flashed her a megawatt, sexy grin.

'If I show you, will you promise to give me an answer?'

'I'll think about it,' she said, biting her lip in mock coyness.

He sprang up and straddled her, the sight of his hard, sex-ready body sending waves of erotic energy cascading through her.

'Okay, well, you'd better start thinking now, because I can't wait any longer— neither to be inside you, nor to get an answer as to whether you want to spend the rest of your life with me.'

She laughed and wrapped her legs around him. She crossed her ankles around his back to lock him in place and pulled him into her already moist body.

'Okay,' he said, breathlessly between thrusts. 'That's one crossed off. What about the other?'

She arched her back and pushed her hips upward to allow him to inch himself deeper into her.

'Of course, I will. I can't *wait* to marry you!'

He locked eyes with her, broke into a broad grin and came in a sudden release of testosterone-fuelled power. A beat later she bucked beneath him in a rush of her own all-consuming pleasure.

She lay back, still panting as her orgasm subsided into a heavenly tingle between her legs, and looked directly at him. She'd noticed he hadn't taken his eyes off her as she'd climaxed, and still seemed entranced. His expression turned serious and there was moisture in his eyes.

'No more waiting, I promise, Seren. I'm never letting you go again.'

'You'd better not,' she said, getting the words out just before he covered her mouth with his.

Without Refuge
By
Annabelle McInnes

Euan sat with his back to a wall, the warmth of the concrete penetrating past the threadbare singlet to his skin. The oppressing heat squeezed the stink of squalor and death from his surroundings. It hovered around him in an invisible cloud of deprecation, a visceral reminder of the primitive foundations that a broken civilisation rested upon. It overwhelmed his senses, coating his tongue in filth and stung his nose. It held most of his focus. That and the ever-increasing violence.

This was meant to be a camp for survivors. A place for refugees to find refuge, food and shelter. Instead, they would more likely find death.

If the plague hadn't killed them, this last remaining stand of society would.

Euan's faculties were trained on the remnants of civility around him. He was exhausted, his circumstances having forced him to remain awake throughout the mayhem. His muscles ached with a continuous thud. His stomach cramped and his tongue felt thick from the limited sustenance and fluid he'd been able to consume. But he would not give up one of the only advantages he had: his location.

A woman screamed. A child wailed. A man grunted in pain while another sobbed. Euan knew that soon there would be no sound. Those who survived would give up, their prayers for mercy going unhindered. The tears shed in grief would be wiped from grubby cheeks. Shoulders would be hunched, knuckles would be bloody, and they would squash the terror that writhed in the pit of their stomach until only the primal need to stay alive remained.

'Got a smoke?' a man asked.

Euan slid his eyes down to the intruder. He hovered below, dirty and unkempt. Hollow cheeks and sunken eyes peered up at him, a human wasting away from lack of security and nourishment. Like they all were.

Like he was.

His focus returned to the mayhem of the open area sprawled out beneath him. The tents erected around concrete buildings had once been the lush green of the tropics, but now the fabric was weathered, faded and torn, coated with a thick layer of dust. They suffered their destruction in a wasteland of sand and stone.

He remained silent.

'Leave him,' another spoke. 'He's been up there for two days. He'll die up there.'

'With smokes?'

'There's no fucking water and you're after cigarettes? Jesus.'

'I want a fucking smoke.'

'Don't speak so loud. They'll hear you.'

There was only a grunt in response. Euan squinted to watch them retreat into the chaos, the glaring beat of the sun highlighting the grease in their matted hair and the angry red sunburn on their exposed grimy skin. Their shoulders were hunched with the need to stay small and unnoticed. Their feet left bare footprints in the dirt.

The game of survival of the fittest had begun. Points were already being placed on the board.

The men before him were going to be on the losing team.

Euan's gaze returned outward, his focus resting on the swirls of dust that alighted with the wind. A gust in his direction forced him to close his eyes, as they stung and precious fluid squeezed from the corners. He clenched his fists, felt his knuckles pop. He sat on his arse, legs bent and spread wide, his hands dangling from the point of each knee. He was tired, so fucking tired. And thirsty. But his desire to survive overrode all his other instincts.

He just had to outlive the others. Then he could scavenge what was left and leave.

The sounds that came next were familiar: flesh meeting flesh, a woman's pleas for mercy, a man's grunts, and a broken wail of despair.

Euan averted his eyes and hardened his heart. He did not intervene.

Survive.

He saw most things now through the eyes of another man. A man whose life hadn't been torn apart by society's breakdown. Who once loved, who once cared. Who once, maybe, would have aided that suffering woman's plight.

But with that decision came consequences. And his goal was survival, life. Not heroics. Not chivalry.

Not death.

He was visible from his ledge but not exposed. The sun only caught him as it made its final descent for the day. The colours of amber, orange, and gold weaved together to create a tapestry of splendour. One of the world's last remaining visible wonders.

That was until he saw him. A striking man running into his territory. Towards the crumbling building. Towards the ledge he sat on.

Euan held his breath and revelled in a moment in time where the dust didn't choke him, where the scent of decay didn't burn his senses. From his height advantage, he could see him clearly. A shock of matted blond hair, a shirtless bronze chest, a square, scruffy jaw. A bruised and swollen eye, a bloodied lip, an arm cradled against a hollowed stomach.

Multiple men ran after their prey.

Euan closed his eyes.

Survive.

Shouts. Grunts. Cries of pain and curse words. Angry accusations and demands.

Survive.

A quick glance. Five against one. That glorious blond hair flying as a straight nose was obliterated under a beefy man's fist.

Blood spraying. Hoots of laughter as the young man fell to

his knees. Boots meeting flesh. A body tumbling about in the dust.

Fucking survive.

A call for a little fun. Belt buckles jangling. Deep male laughter. A final attempt at retaliation. The crunch of bone.

Silence from a perfect, bloody body in the dirt.

Fuck.

Euan heaved himself upright. His muscles screamed and his bones throbbed as he pulled his shoulders back and lifted his chin. He looked down from the ledge he occupied, the single point of advantage in this cesspool of depravity.

But it wasn't his only one.

'Holy shit, that guy's huge!'

'Look at all those tattoos, Christ.'

'I'm getting outta here, lads. No pretty boy is worth what that monster will do to you. I heard he hospitalised three men before the army left.'

'I heard six.'

Standing, Euan felt light-headed. He waited for the sensation to pass. It didn't. Getting down was going to require him to jump, but he liked his unbroken ankles a lot more than he liked his pride. He stepped to the edge, squatted, took the fractured concrete ledge in his hands and pushed his feet out.

He dangled.

Five men took two steps back.

He let go.

Two men fled.

He hit the dirt, falling to his haunches.

One man cursed as another spat.

He rose slowly, pulling his body upright.

Three men fled.

Euan curled his lip in disgust.

It was a strange sensation to walk. To place one foot in front of the other. To remain vertical after not having eaten in a week, or consumed water in over two days. His fingers tingled. His tongue felt swollen. His steps were slow. Fatigue weighed on him heavily, an oppressive cloak made from cement and sand. Even to draw breath into his lungs required conscious thought.

But he had to be quick. Those men would be back and they

would bring others.

He stopped when he reached the body, a desperate thrum starting to vibrate in his chest. His arms were at his side in a stance of relaxation, but Euan was not comfortable. Every muscle was tensed, every sense on alert.

He pressed his lips together. He knew he didn't have the energy to get involved.

But how could he not?

Beautiful in feature, beautiful in form, it was obvious why the young man had been targeted; he was prettier than most of the women who still lived.

'You still got your boots,' the bloody man croaked as he cracked his eyes open to stare at Euan's feet.

'You got your arse kicked,' was the stoic reply.

'They took my watch.'

'You lost your watch.'

'I want it back.'

'You should want to live more.'

The silence that followed was heavy with wordless, stubborn defiance.

Euan clenched his jaw and scanned his surroundings. He didn't like this angle. Didn't like being on the ground. Everything was worse from this viewpoint. Especially the smell.

'You're the biggest man I've ever seen. And you have a lot of ink.'

The comment was ignored. 'You gonna get up?'

'You gonna help me get my watch?'

Euan sucked his teeth. He could hear footsteps. The rumble of male voices. The clink of weapons.

The wind blew, the dust cleared, and Euan saw the glint of steel and smear of wood against a filthy human backdrop.

The final tether on civility had snapped. This was the end of everything.

'Can you run?' he asked.

The man sat up, long fingers touching a split lip, a bruised eye, a swollen jaw. He wiggled his bare toes. 'I can run,' he said.

'Then let's go.'

'To the ledge? We'll be trapped there. They'll kill us.'

Euan shook his head. His short hair enabled the hot sun to

burn the tips of his ears. 'Not to the ledge. We're getting out of here. There's nothing left.'

'But they said we needed to wait. They said they would come back.'

Euan grabbed the man's shoulders and pulled him to his feet, drawing him close. Their noses brushed, breath intermingled. Euan's gaze held eyes the colour of jade. 'They're not coming back. They're all likely dead too. We stay, we die. We leave, we live. You decide.'

'You'll help me get my watch back?' the man asked, his teeth tarnished with blood.

'You gonna go after it even if I don't?' Euan replied.

He watched as jade glinted. A furrow between two blond eyebrows eased, and a shit-eating grin split across a bearded face. 'Yes.'

Euan was startled by the brilliance of that smile. He shook his head and grunted in annoyance at himself. 'You gonna run?'

'You gonna keep up?'

'Just go, kid.'

A burst of unfettered laughter. 'Just follow, big guy.'

~ * ~

There were knees.

Knees that were attached to bronze, muscular thighs. Thighs that were parted, naked. In a world where mayhem and anarchy reigned, naked knees and parted thighs were going to be Euan's final undoing.

Because these naked knees ultimately led to a naked cock. A long, smooth, thick naked cock. A naked cock that currently sat at rest in a nest of honey-blond curls.

'I can put my pants back on.'

'The blood—'

'Can probably be cleaned with my pants on.'

'Probably, not properly.'

Suddenly, inspecting the wounds on dusty, muscular calves became vital.

'It makes you uncomfortable.'

It did make Euan uncomfortable, but not in the way the man likely suspected. The tingle in his fingers had dissipated, but not the acute sensitivity. His nausea had settled, but not the tumultuous churn in the pit of his gut. His senses were no longer strained, but he remained overwhelmed.

Every part of his body, mind and soul yearned for the man he tended.

So yeah, he was uncomfortable. But he was not deterred.

'I've seen a cock before.'

The man chuckled. 'Have you?'

Euan's response was deadpan—and idiotically unnecessary. 'I have one.'

That chuckle became a reverberation of laughter.

Euan let his hands drop. He rose, turned his back to the man and pretended that the heat that enflamed his cheeks was due to the warmth of the tin hovel they hid in.

'The blood is gone. Cuts are shallow. Can you walk?'

'I ran here, remember?'

Euan could hear the smirk. 'I remember,' he muttered.

He'd never forget it. He'd been perched on his ledge for two days. Two days was an eternity to the remnants of humanity. Two days was the difference between dying of thirst, starvation or bacteria. Two days was enough to lose hope. It was enough to see children perish, loved ones succumb to a disease that had no cure, only a natural immunity that could save you.

'Hand me my pants.'

Euan averted his eyes while the man dressed, looking toward the camp they'd left behind. The dust rose like a tornado of despair, the sorrow of humankind taking physical form and reaching for the heavens, carrying lost souls, desperate for their master.

The man moved to his side. They stood shoulder to shoulder, both gazes peering out of a sliver of light between the tin sheeting. 'Name's Nicholas Sutherland. Nick.'

'Euan.'

'Last name?'

'Does it matter?'

Euan tried not to look, but he felt the pull as if it were a physical tether, drawing his attention to Nick at his side. In the end, only his eyes moved, but his focus was snagged. A flash of glossy bronze skin that was almost iridescent in the muted shadows. Tense, delineated muscles danced with each minute shift. A swollen nose marred a potentially faultless profile. A golden beard that complemented another wiry nest of blond curls.

'The watch was my dad's. It's all I've got. I want it back.'

Euan's gaze reluctantly returned toward the setting sun. He squinted. 'You'll probably die trying to get it back.'

'Does it matter?'

Euan turned his head then, his full focus now riveted on Nick. His height had him looking down, but not as far as most men. He didn't answer. He couldn't.

Putting a voice to the words that echoed inside his mind was too terrifying to comprehend.

It does.

Nick remained motionless. 'I thought the army took all the guns with them when they left.'

Euan mirrored his static stance and turned his gaze back toward the sliver of sunlight. 'There are always men with guns.'

The silence that followed was poignant. Euan sensed Nick struggling with what he wanted to say next. He didn't prompt him, just waited, his chest expanding with every breath. Each inhalation drew in the scent of not just the stink of a dank hovel, but of honey-blond hair and glimmering bronze skin. The scent of man, of musk, of masculine exertions and sweat.

Euan stopped breathing through his nose.

'You didn't have to jump in, you know. I had it sorted.'

Euan held in the instinctual snort of disbelief. 'They would have killed you if I hadn't.'

'Nah.' Nick waved the warning off.

'They would have done far worse than just kill you,' he reiterated.

The reply was hesitant. 'They were just messing around.'

Euan swallowed. 'No, they weren't.'

Nick breathed in deeply. He held the oxygen in his lungs for long moments. Euan wondered what he smelled as he drew in the air, so close to his own sweat-dampened body.

'Thanks,' Nick whispered.

Euan wet his dry lips and crossed his arms against his chest. 'We'll wait until dark.'

140

The response was low, and Euan caught the impulsive glance his way. 'Okay.'

~ * ~

'This will definitely get us killed.'

'We're going to die anyway, right?'

Darkness enveloped them. They'd relocated from the tin lean-to in the late afternoon closer to the camp. Euan could only see the shimmer of firelight in Nick's eyes, the flames too far away to light the features of his face.

'You'll owe me,' he said, dismissing the effect those eager eyes had on his disposition.

'I'm okay with that,' Nick replied, the sudden deepening of his voice tying knots inside Euan's stomach.

Survive.

It was too late for that now. He was heading into the dragon's den with nothing but his fists and wits to keep his heart beating in his chest. To keep the heart beating in the chest of the man who crouched at his side. Still shirtless, still striking.

Still masculine.

'Okay, so you distract them with the rocks. I'll get the watch.'

Euan shook off his lack of focus. 'Do you remember who took it?'

Nick's 'yeah' was heavy with unsaid meaning.

Euan rubbed his grimy hands along his thighs. His legs ached from lingering in the crouched position for most of the evening. 'This is a fucking terrible plan.'

Nick snorted. 'You were the one who sat in silence all afternoon.'

He had. And he didn't lament it. If he had put words to the tempest that raged inside his mind, he would have said something he regretted. He felt a mix of lust and terror surge inside him. He was meant to be selfish, looking after his own life. These impulsive actions and rash plans would see them both dead.

But then Nick would shift, the waning limited light glancing off his chest. His shirtless torso had rippled. His toned abdominals had flexed and his pectoral muscles had stretched and contracted.

And Euan's mouth had gone dry.

He was at war. A war within himself without a victor. Silence had been the best outcome for everyone.

'Ready?' Nick asked.

'No.' But he stood up anyway. His muscles groaned. He almost let the audible complaint past his lips, but he bit it back. For some foolish reason, he didn't want Nick to think him an old man, even though Euan was sure he was at least ten years Nick's senior.

Survive.

Instincts honed by an innate desire to live and years of training sharpened, forcing him to concentrate. 'You go around the back. Try and not get their attention. We're more likely to get out alive if we only attack the man who has the watch. There were at least ten earlier.'

'But they're all hungry, tired and shit. That's the equivalent of five, maybe six.'

'*We* are hungry, tired and shit. How many does that make us?'

'We'll be fine. You count for at least three.'

'It won't make a difference. Groups make men stupid. Just get the watch and get out, yeah?'

'You're no fun.'

'Just get the fucking watch, Nick.'

'Fine.'

Euan swallowed the sudden surge of fear that clawed up his throat as he watched Nick move out from their hiding place.

The glimmer of Nick's blond hair disappeared into the maze of midnight green fabric. A lean body bent low to remain unseen, flames highlighting the muscles of his toned physique. Euan had the urge to run after him, pull him back to safety, back to his side. To hold him, have his warm skin press against his own. Have the smell of man fill and overwhelm his senses.

Survive.

He took a step back. He thought of retreating, leaving the young man to his own foolishness and reckless ideas.

Then there was a shout of warning. Before Euan realised his own actions, he was standing and throwing a rock in a campfire.

A burst of spark and flame had men swearing and falling back from the flares. A woman cried out in pain.

Euan threw another rock.

Demands to find the culprit. Bellows of anger, rage and irritation.

Then Nick's blond head popping up into the fray.

Fucking idiot.

From where he crouched, he couldn't hear what was said, but he could guess. There were two options: move forward into the light or back into the shadows. Euan's thundering heart would only let him take one.

He walked with purpose to the growing skirmish. When the first man attempted to take a swing at him, he snatched the hand out of the air and twisted until a shoulder popped and an elbow crunched.

A holler of agony filled the night and a writhing body crumpled to the ground.

Euan scanned his surroundings. The fire showcased what Nick had predicted—a group of starving men, ragged and desperate. They raged with the fury of adrenaline and fear. This was not an organised cohort; these unwashed husbands, sons, and brothers were now simply thugs and thieves. They were not even worth Euan's escalated breath.

Another man approached. Euan used skill to jab him in the face and break only his nose. He fell back with a cry.

When another tried to attack, he utilised his expertise to apply just enough power behind a fist to force the man to the ground unconscious, but not to his death.

He was no murderer.

There were shouts for retreat. The fire spat and hissed, the flames creating shadows of light against the dark. Bodies scrambled in the dust. Then a blond man leaped over the flames in a show of youthful bravado and exuberance. A gold watch was held high.

Euan wiped his bloody hands on his jeans, his brows pulling tightly together in extremely mature annoyance. But the tight steel band that had crushed his chest loosened at the sight.

'You were a boxer!' Nick exclaimed as they began to retreat.

Euan spat onto the dirt.

'Heavyweight? No wonder you're the size of a tank. Is that what all your tattoos are for? To show off how many men you've taken down?'

Euan couldn't hold in the irritated growl that rumbled deep inside his chest.

'You're so badass.'

'You're lucky to be alive. We should get out of here.'

'We should.'

But Euan was forced to stop when Nick moved into his path. A dark shape that blocked the inky blackness that led to safety behind him. 'What are you doing? We need to go. Now.'

Hands were at Euan's neck. Warm masculine hands. A firm grip held him still, but his shock kept him that way.

His mouth opened. He thought to scold, but then firm lips were pressing to his. The intoxicating scent of male sweat flooded his senses. A wet tongue brushed his lips, demanding entry. The hands at his neck firmed, tightening their grip. He jerked when a naked, hard chest pressed against his. The thin cotton of his singlet was the only thing separating the tantalising concept of skin touching skin.

That tongue pushed past Euan's lips and it was then that he noticed what has happening below their waistbands. Blood was flooding an organ that should not have been getting aroused.

He was getting hard. Over a man.

Euan reared back, breaking free from Nick's hold. It was instinct that had him clench his fist and slam it into the side of Nick's face.

He didn't think why he held back just enough of his strength not to kill the bastard. He didn't consider the reason behind why he purposely missed the soft temple that would have killed him. He didn't reflect on the sudden surge of guilt that almost had him bending over and plucking Nick out of the dust.

All he thought about was how his cock throbbed, how his heart ached.

He turned and stormed into the night.

A muttered 'you could have just said no' twisted his conscience as he left.

~ * ~

Euan sat in the darkness. His back rested against a rock, still warm from the heat of the sun. He didn't know how long he'd crouched in the sand, but he did know it would soon be morning.

Survive.

It had been his single mantra. A prayer to himself after he watched countless die. He knew that once the government had collapsed, society would dissolve and only those with the strength, stamina and fortitude to endure in a dystopian world would be the ones to survive.

But maybe there was more to life than just survival. Maybe a man couldn't live without the most fundamental of human needs.

Needs that sustained the soul rather than just the body.

Needs that didn't have to come from a woman.

Needs like affection, tenderness, forgiveness, compassion.

Needs like love.

Euan stood, rubbed a calloused hand over a rugged beard and blinked back toward the remaining flickering lights. He didn't have to think about where he needed to go.

He found Nick sitting against the side of the tin shanty.

'I heard there are houses out west that are self-sufficient. Set up to last off the grid. They'll probably all be abandoned, their owners dead.'

Even in the darkness, Nick's smile was blinding. 'You came back.'

'I hear they get rain there too.'

'You came back.'

'I don't want your death on my conscience.'

'You came back.'

Euan let his jaw relax and his fists unclench. 'I came back.'

Nick rose, his lithe body shifting with the grace of a cheetah. He walked until he stood before Euan, a form as glorious and perfect as Michelangelo's *David*.

Euan licked his lips and tried not to shuffle his feet.

He ignored the sweat that warmed his palms.

But he didn't disregard the lengthening of his cock at the sight of such magnificence.

Nick took Euan's cheeks in his hands, but the invitation was too tender. Euan didn't know what Nick enjoyed, what experience he had. But he did know his own desires, his own needs.

And he desired dominance.

A quick yank and Nick's back was pressed against Euan's front. Euan held a fistful of those glorious honey-blond locks in his hand. He forced Nick's head back, arching his neck so he could feast on the exposed corded throat.

Nick groaned from the involuntary vulnerability. Euan couldn't help the instinctual need to bare his teeth and press the visible canines into the muscle. He thrust his hips, his engorged cock rubbing against the crease of Nick's arse through the fabric of their pants.

Nick grunted when Euan bit. He gasped when Euan pinched one flat nipple with his free hand, then groaned when Euan combined the pain of both with the incessant thrusting of his hips against a body held immobile by his strength.

'You done this before?'

Nick tried to nod. 'Yeah. You?'

There was a moment that Euan fought two sides of himself. He could remain an enigma, a man without emotion, filled with only a rampant desire and chauvinist ideals. Then there was his inner self—far more honest, but far more vulnerable.

'Yeah,' he breathed. 'But not with a man.'

'Christ.'

'Is it the same?'

Nick choked out a laugh, pulled from Euan's hold and forced his face close until their lips brushed. 'A little. But with one major difference.'

He kissed Euan then. It was aggressive, passionate. He bit his lips while tugging and tearing at Euan's jeans with a desperation that boarded on insanity.

Euan gripped two fistfuls of Nick's hair and pulled. 'What's that?' he demanded.

Nick's teeth were visible. 'You can be rougher.'

Then he pushed.

Caught off guard, Euan fell to his arse in the dirt. Before he could scramble to his feet, Nick was upon him. They grappled, wrestled for superiority. Euan didn't only have the bulk needed to hold Nick down, he also had the wrestling training. Before long, Nick was pinned beneath him, his arse in the air, while Euan frantically pulled at the one piece of clothing Nick wore.

'How should I—'

'Spit. Use spit.'

'Fuck,' Euan groaned, then spat on his palm.

He rubbed the slippery liquid up and down his heavy, engorged shaft.

Nick tried to twist in Euan's hold, but he held fast, grinning at the wicked pleasure of power that surged through him.

Euan positioned himself, spat once more in Nick's crease and began to push.

'Christ,' Nick hissed. 'You big there too?'

Euan huffed. 'No one has complained before. Slower?'

'Yeah.'

Euan let his hold loosen, but he didn't shift his weight. His body pushed Nick farther into the dirt, and he covered those beautiful muscles with his own. He didn't question his motives when he bent and tenderly kissed the sensitive spot behind Nick's ear.

The answering groan let Euan know he was good to continue.

He pressed his hips forward, tiny thrusts that forced his cock into the warm, welcoming heat of Nick's body.

The man trembled underneath him, his forehead pressed to the sand, his nails biting into the arm that banded around his chest.

One more forceful thrust and he penetrated beyond that tight ring of muscle.

Euan groaned and Nick hissed, following with a deep guttural moan that had a feral grin splitting across Euan's face.

'You like that?' He pulled out, thrust again.

Nick's answering growl was all the response Euan required.

He lost it, lost himself to the feeling, the sensations, the physical wonder of feeling pleasure in the body of another man.

He felt Nick vibrate beneath him and suspected he was dry-humping gravel. He pulled himself from Nick, smiling at the distressed moan that came from the loss, and shifted until Nick was on his hands and knees. Euan rose behind him and positioned himself back at Nick's entrance. He thrust home.

The guttural grunt that rumbled from them both echoed through the craggy wasteland. Euan reached around and, with the precision of a desperate man, grasped Nick's turgid cock and pumped that magnificent organ in time with his own plunges.

They almost came together, with Nick finishing a moment earlier. His desperate thrusts into Euan's hand, forcing himself to take more of Euan's cock into his body as he did so, pushed Euan over the edge.

Euan collapsed over Nick and both men crumbled to the dirt, their panting breaths loud in the night air.

'I like rough,' Euan muttered.

Nick huffed out a bite of laughter. 'I like the idea of going west.'

Euan's lips twitched. 'I like the idea of company. But you follow my lead, yeah? No more half-cocked plans.'

Nick snorted, rolled out from under Euan and shifted until he could pull his pants up.

They both stared up into the sky. Stars dotted the infinite blackness. The silence they shared was comfortable. Their sweat-soaked bodies were covered in dust, their knees bloody.

'We need water,' Nick croaked.

'We need to survive,' Euan replied.

'Together?' Nick asked.

'Yeah.'

The Lady and the Libertine
By
Amy Rose Bennett

St Ives House, Cavendish Square, London, May 1812

'I want you to ruin me.'

Lady Angelina Pemberton held her breath, waiting for Justin Huntingdon, Lord St Ives, to react to her bold, completely mad request. She had no idea how she'd summoned the nerve to visit the viscount's townhouse so late at night, but desperate times called for desperate measures. And she was desperate indeed.

The indecently handsome viscount opened his mouth and shut it again. He took several steps towards her, across the drawing room rug, then paused and raked a hand through his negligently tousled, dark blond hair. Crossing his arms over his wide chest, he eyed her like she'd just escaped from Bedlam, which didn't auger well for what she had in mind.

'You want me to ruin you?' he said carefully. His voice was deep with a seductive rasp as if he'd just woken from sleep. And perhaps he had, given that he wore buff breeches, top boots, an open-necked cambric shirt, and a burgundy silk banyan. It was not the attire a gentleman usually wore when meeting titled young ladies. But then, there was nothing 'usual' about this situation.

Mustering what was left of her courage, Angelina drew a fortifying breath. 'Yes.'

Lord St Ives narrowed his topaz brown eyes. 'Two thoughts

spring to mind. Why? And why me?'

'Well, the answer to your second question should be rather obvious given your reputation, my lord. Since you resigned your commission as a naval officer six years ago, you've become one of London's worst rakehells. A legendary scoundrel. A debaucher of women. A libertine.' Angelina managed a small smile despite the wild fluttering inside her belly. 'Or so the rumours go.'

The viscount gave a sardonic smile. 'Because all rumours must be true.'

'There's no smoke without fire.' She was fairly certain Lord St Ives was the wicked Tattooed Viscount whose amorous exploits frequently appeared in the scandal sheets so she added, 'I've even heard you have a tattoo.'

'Would you like to see it?' With a wolfish grin he loosened the tie of his banyan and began to pull his shirt from his breeches.

'No!' she cried, but not before she'd caught a glimpse of taut abdominal muscles. Good Lord, the man was well-made. The *ton* gossipmongers had declared he was devilishly handsome and a lover like no other. But none of the rumours mentioned he had the physique of a Roman warrior—tall, lean, and muscular.

Lord St Ives laughed, clearly amused by her shocked reaction. 'So you don't *really* want me to ruin you,' he said, prowling dangerously closer.

Angelina willed herself to hold her ground. Confidence was the key to making this plan work. 'Well I do, but being here alone with you tonight should do the trick. Your notoriety is enough to ruin me.'

'Guilt by association,' he remarked, but he didn't seem insulted by the idea given the twinkle in his eyes.

'Yes.'

Lord St Ives took another step closer and she caught the heady scent of his cologne. Something spicy and musky. Sandalwood, perhaps? 'As intrigued as I am by your charming proposal, Lady Angelina, you still haven't told me why.'

Angelina squared her shoulders, preparing to make her case. She needed to keep her wits about her. 'My betrothal to Baron Wexford was recently announced. And given he is older than

Methuselah, more pious than a priest, and lives in the middle of nowhere—in a draft-ridden castle in Ireland—when Parliament isn't sitting, I do not wish to marry him, despite what my father, Lord Middleham, has decreed. If my reputation is sullied, I am confident Lord Wexford will look elsewhere for a wife.'

'And perhaps many other gentlemen will. The label of "ruined woman" is a difficult burden to bear.'

'It's a risk I'm willing to take.'

The gold in Lord St Ives's topaz eyes flared. 'I don't usually *sully* debutantes. But I might be tempted to make an exception.'

Angelina swallowed, resisting the urge to pick up her yellow silk skirts and flee. She suddenly felt like a tasty morsel in the path of a hungry lion. 'However, as I explained, I'm not really asking you to.'

Lord St Ives flashed a mischievous smile. 'Aren't you curious? To see what all the fuss is about? You may as well be hung for a sheep as a lamb. Me too for that matter.'

'No. I'm not curious in the slightest,' said Angelina firmly. Quite unexpectedly, it seemed she needed to convince herself as much as Lord St Ives. 'Besides, what possible harm could come to you?'

The viscount retreated and rested a well-muscled arm along the mantelpiece. 'The reason I stay away from debutantes, my dear, is that I'm loath to deal with irate fathers. I don't wish to be called out or forced into marriage because I've compromised someone's daughter. I'm not the marrying kind.'

'Yet I hear you seduce married women,' she countered. 'What about irate husbands?'

'Very well then. Virgins are not to my taste.'

Angelina arched a brow. 'Yet a moment ago, you said you might be tempted to...' She bit her lip. Oh dear, why had she said that?

Interest sparked in Lord St Ives's eyes. 'Yes, I did, didn't I?' he said, rubbing his lean jaw. 'If I choose to go along with your risky plan, I think you need to make it worth my while.'

'You require payment?' Angelina's gaze darted to her reticule which sat on a nearby occasional table. She had a few guineas...

'I don't need money, my dear.'

'Let me assure you, it's not *that* risky. My father is too old to call anyone out. And a hopeless shot. I thought if I simply stayed here all night, then left in the morning, not too early, but early enough for others to notice, it wouldn't take too long for the rumours to reach my father's and Lord Wexford's ears. And *voilà*, no more engagement.'

'You're really that desperate to avoid marriage to Wexford that you would risk destroying your reputation forevermore? Because that's what will happen.'

Angelina raised her chin. 'I'd rather die a shrivelled up old maid than marry that old goat. His hair is turning grey and his teeth are yellow. And did I mention he's pious? He reads from the Scriptures every night.'

'Hmm. He sounds absolutely frightful. Although it's a shame not to make the most of this evening...' Lord St Ives focused on her mouth.

Oh my. Angelina had the overwhelming urge to lick her dry lips. 'I appreciate your offer, but I must respectfully decline. I assume you have a spare guest room?'

'Yes. Several.' The viscount's disconcerting gaze raked over her body before returning to her eyes. 'However, we still haven't settled on what incentive you're prepared to offer.'

Angelina stiffened. 'A gentleman wouldn't—'

'Ah, sweeting,' he said in dark voice. 'We both know, I'm not a gentleman.'

Before Angelina could draw another breath, Lord St Ives had closed the distance between them. He lifted her chin with gentle fingers. 'What will you give me to spend the night here?' he murmured, his warm breath caressing her lips.

His meaning was clear. And God help her, Angelina actually did want to acquiesce. If this was her only opportunity to be kissed, *really* kissed, why shouldn't she offer Lord St Ives what he wanted? Part of her—a wicked part—had always longed to experience physical love with a handsome man. How many times had she envied other debutantes flirting with rakehells at balls this Season whilst her mother watched her like a hawk? The odious Lord Wexford barely regarded her. If damnation awaited her, surely she should have a little fun before she got there?

'Very well,' she whispered. Delicious tremors of anticipation shivered across her skin. 'You may have a kiss. That is all.'

He smiled. 'We have a deal, Lady Angelina.' His thumb softly brushed over her trembling lower lip. 'Have you ever been kissed before?'

'No.'

'Ah, I'm honoured then.' One of his large hands slid around to her lower back, drawing her closer. Male heat, hotter than the fire in the nearby grate, radiated from him. 'A first kiss should be special. It should stop your heart, steal your breath, and melt your bones.'

'It sounds positively fatal.' Angelina placed her hands against Lord St Ives's hard-as-marble chest. Even though the sensible part of her thought to push him away, her reckless side made her push her hips against him like a wanton during a waltz.

She bit her lip. Was she really going to do this? Allow herself to be kissed by the infamous Tattooed Viscount? What remained of her reason compelled her to ask, 'Would a handshake suffice?'

'It would be poor form to renege on our agreement, my lady,' Lord St Ives murmured, his attention now completely focused on her mouth. He angled his head and cupped her face with a gentle hand. He leaned imperceptibly closer. 'You can let me know at the end what you think.'

Her breath quickening, Angelina closed her eyes as Lord St Ives's mouth descended. His lips were soft yet firm and tasted faintly of brandy as they brushed against hers in a slow, teasing glide. When the tip of his tongue boldly slipped between her lips she gasped with shock and he ventured farther, stroking and exploring, tasting her thoroughly, coaxing her to explore him with her own tongue in return.

She'd never imagined a kiss could be like this, so wicked yet so good. Addictively good. Like hot chocolate or champagne. Indeed, the warm, wild rush of desire through her veins made her dizzy, as if she'd drunk too much wine and she sagged against Lord St Ives's long hard body, her hands tangling clumsily in the thick silky hair at his nape.

But he didn't seem to mind; if anything, he lashed her closer and even though she was an innocent, she recognised the feel of his arousal pressing into her belly. She was in the lion's den of

London's worst rakehell and she should be terrified—but she wasn't. All she felt was exhilaration and a deep ache inside her, a need for something more...

She broke away, breathless and boneless just as Lord St Ives had stated she should feel after her first kiss. Except for one thing.

'You were wrong... about my heart,' she murmured. 'It didn't stop. It's racing. So very fast. And,' she inhaled a shaky breath as she caught his hot golden gaze. 'I think... I actually do want you to ruin me. In truth.'

Lord St Ives searched her eyes. 'Are you certain?'

Angelina nodded and reached up to trace a trembling finger along his wide sensuous mouth. 'Yes. If I am to be shunned by polite society, and regarded by most as unfit for marriage, I may as well have something to reminisce about in my dotage. Besides...' She boldly slid a hand beneath the hem of his shirt. 'I am eager to see your tattoo.'

~*~

Justin couldn't quite believe it. Had this impudent chit really just asked him to take her innocence? It appeared she had, considering her slender hand was resting against his naked abdomen just above the waistband of his breeches.

When his butler had invaded his private study a short time ago to announce the Earl of Middleham's daughter wanted to see him about 'an urgent matter,' he'd cursed the heavens. His quiet night in—a rarity of an occurrence—had been ruined. But now... now as he examined the delectable, golden-haired woman in his arms, her full lips all wet and bruised from his kiss, and her lovely green eyes all drowsy with arousal, he rather thought he'd been blessed with good fortune. His cock, which had already begun to twitch during their kiss, began to swell in earnest at the thought of taking her.

One thing was certain, deflowering Lady Angelina Pemberton would be infinitely more diverting than drinking brandy as he played a solitary game of chess.

However, by the time they reached his bedchamber, Angelina was worrying her bottom lip with her teeth. 'You can change your mind, you know,' he said gently. He prayed that she wouldn't. There was something about this young woman that tugged at him in the oddest way, making this encounter acutely poignant. Perhaps it was the uncertainty of Angelina's smile. Her vulnerability. He was, quite unexpectedly, touched.

She offered a tremulous smile. 'I'm absolutely sure I want to do this. With you. After all, you're a master of seduction.'

He inclined his head. 'Thank you. I trust I won't disappoint.'

'I'm sure you won't.'

'Come.' Taking her hand, Justin led Angelina farther into the room towards his bed—a huge, carved walnut affair with a royal blue velvet canopy edged with gold silk. Branches of candles burned brightly on the matching walnut mantelpiece and a fire glowed in the grate.

Pausing by the footboard, Justin gently drew Angelina into his arms. He wondered how much she knew about bed sport. Probably next to nothing considering the fact she was biting her poor abused lower lip again.

'Shouldn't we snuff out the candles?' she whispered.

Justin flashed his rake's smile, hoping to light her desire again. 'But then you wouldn't be able to see my tattoo.'

'Oh, right... Yes.' Angelina sat on the velvet padded bench at the end of his bed, her back ramrod straight. 'Very well,' she said grimly as if she were about to face the lash not her lover. 'I'm ready.'

Locking his gaze with hers, Justin shed his banyan then his shirt, exposing his upper body. He was comfortable in his own skin. Because he rode, fenced, and boxed regularly, he'd maintained the physique he'd developed during his years as a captain serving in His Majesty's Royal Navy. His disrobing had the desired effect; Angelina's frown had gone and her lovely green eyes had darkened with want.

Her rapt expression fuelled his own lust; his cock jerked and thickened, tenting his breeches. When she rose and gently touched his left pectoral muscle where the tattoo of a sword-wielding lion rampant and a bloodied heart lay, he couldn't bite back a groan.

'You are beautiful,' she breathed, tracing the lines of the tattoo, making his nipples pebble. Her gaze lifted to his, searching. 'You must have been in so much pain when you got this.'

Justin shrugged. 'It only hurt a little.'

Angelina frowned. 'You mistake my meaning. Someone—a woman—broke your heart. Didn't she?'

Justin drew an unsteady breath, amazed by Angelina's perceptiveness. And her tenderness. No one had ever discerned the meaning behind his tattoo. He'd chosen the design to forever remind him that seven years ago, his faithless fiancée had cut out his heart whilst he was at sea, fighting Napoleon's fleet. But Angelina didn't need to know that. 'It was a long time ago,' he said simply, attempting to lighten the moment.

'I'm sorry. I shouldn't have said anything.' Angelina withdrew her hand but Justin caught it and brought it to his lips.

'Don't be,' he murmured roughly.

'No, it was rude of me. I spoke without thinking. But I did mean what I said first. You are truly beautiful.'

'As are you.' Justin lowered his head and claimed her mouth. Within moments Angelina was kissing him back with equal ardour; her tongue danced with his as she pressed her breasts against his naked chest. His cock throbbed, fit to burst. 'Let me see you,' he whispered against her hot, sweet mouth. 'Let me show you pleasures that you'll never forget.'

'Oh. You want me to undress?'

Angelina's forehead had knitted into a frown. Justin drew back. 'If you don't want to, I'm sure we can work with that too.'

She smiled with endearing shyness. 'You must think me gauche and tiresome compared to your usual lovers.'

'Not at all. In fact, you're rather refreshing.' Threading his fingers through hers, he led her to the fireside and bade her sit beside him upon a settee upholstered in gold damask. 'I thought you might prefer if we moved away from the bed.'

'Thank you.' She folded her hands in her lap as if she were about to take tea with him, not make love. 'What now, my lord?'

He smiled. 'So formal,' he said with a reassuring smile. 'Before we proceed any further you must agree to use my given name, Justin.'

She inclined her head. 'Very well, as long as you call me Angelina.'

'Well then, Angelina. May I take down your hair?'

'Of course.' She turned and Justin carefully removed the pins until her thick golden locks cascaded about her slender shoulders. He gently swept her hair to one side and placed a whisper-soft kiss on her elegant neck. How sweet she smelled; the delicate scent of her floral perfume and the underlying fragrance of her skin made his need spiral. She was delectable. An angel indeed.

Somehow keeping his baser urges in check, he gently gathered her close and kissed her, softly but deeply until she was moaning and breathless. When her hands stroked over his naked chest and shoulders, he knew it was time to take things further. Cupping one of her breasts, he teased her nipple through her clothing with his thumb.

Angelina gasped, breaking the kiss. 'Heavens, that's...' Her fingernails raked across his back as he continued to taunt the rigid nub. 'Oh, my goodness...'

'Do you want me to stop?' Christ, he hoped not.

'No. In fact...' A crimson blush stained Angelina's cheeks. 'I think I'd like you to undo my gown.'

'With pleasure.' With a few deft movements, Justin loosened Angelina's yellow silk bodice, stays, and chemise, exposing her perfect breasts. High and round, tipped with dark rosy nipples, they gleamed liked ivory in the firelight. Justin licked his lips. Sweet Jesus, she was good enough to eat and he intended to have his fill.

Pulling Angelina across his lap, he lowered his head and flicked one taut pink bud with his tongue before surrounding it with his lips and suckling. He plucked lightly at the other nipple and it wasn't long before Angelina was clutching his shoulders and whimpering with pleasure. He gave a soft growl when she began to squirm against his straining erection. It was the most exquisite of tortures but he was determined to please Angelina before he sought his own release.

When he was certain Angelina must be wet and wanting more, he raised his head and murmured thickly, 'You have such very pretty tits, my sweet angel. I'd wager you have a pretty cunny as well.'

Angelina blinked as if waking from a dream. 'You... you want to see my...?'

'Your cunny. Your quim.' His hand slid beneath her skirts and caressed the bare flesh above her stocking. 'But more than that, I'd love to stroke it and kiss it until you break apart in ecstasy. If you'll let me.'

A blush washed over Angelina's face, down her neck, all the way to the tips of her delightful breasts. 'I know so little about lovemaking.'

'Trust me. You'll enjoy this.' Justin slid to the hearthrug and gently pushed Angelina's skirts up her slender legs until the dark blonde thatch between her thighs was revealed. His nostrils flared as he caught the musky scent of her arousal. 'Lean back and open your legs for me, sweetheart.'

~ * ~

Angelina's face burned as she spread her legs, exposing her most private part to Justin's hungry gaze. She couldn't quite believe that London's most renowned lover was about to pleasure her in such a wicked and most singular way. At the same time, it was strangely exhilarating—the most wild and thrilling thing she'd ever done.

Justin gently pushed her legs even wider and she closed her eyes. *Oh, God.* She clutched the silk cushions scattered around her. The insistent pulse in her quim was unbearable but she trusted Justin would be able to relieve her agony.

Justin's fingers ruffled the curls hiding her sex then his lips touched her inner thigh. She dared to peek at him through her eyelashes, watching in rapt fascination as he blew across her damp, vulnerable folds. Hot shivers danced over her skin and she whimpered with frustration. 'Please,' she implored, 'I need...'

'Shhh, my angel. I know exactly what you need.' One of Justin's wicked fingers slid along the wet seam of her sex until he found an excruciatingly sensitive spot at the apex. A low moan escaped her as he began to circle the tight bud. Without thinking, she arched her hips and opened wider, inviting him to explore further.

Spreading her tender flesh with his thumbs, at last Justin placed his mouth on her and she gasped at the sinfully exquisite sensation. He pleasured her delicate peak, his tongue flicking and swirling, darting and licking, driving her wild. Pushing her towards something she couldn't name, something just out of reach. Something she wanted so badly it hurt.

As if sensing her acute need, Justin suckled delicately on her core... and then that strange, elusive *something* burst to life deep inside her. Pulsating, glorious pleasure rushed through her veins and she melted into the silk cushions of the settee, breathless and overwhelmed. Replete.

When Justin gathered her into his arms and kissed her, grateful tears welled in her eyes. 'Thank you,' she whispered. 'What you did... it was absolute bliss. You are wonderful and I will never forget this. Thank you.'

Justin's mouth lifted into a satisfied smile. With his golden-brown hair completely dishevelled, he reminded Angelina of a well-fed lion. 'You're very welcome, sweetheart. I'm thrilled you've experienced true pleasure.'

Angelina frowned as a realisation struck her. 'But what about you? You haven't...' she gestured at his breeches where his member still strained. 'Do you want to put yourself inside me? I've heard that's what men do...'

Justin shook his head. 'It would be unfair of me to take your maidenhead. Or get you with child. Despite what you think, I'm certain that you will wed one day and have lots of beautiful babies.'

Angelina traced along the blade of his aristocratic nose, then the line of his chiselled lips. When he playfully nipped at her fingertip, she laughed. For a wicked libertine, he was really rather sweet. 'I'm sure you will have beautiful babies too.'

Justin chuckled. 'Perhaps one day. But for now...' He drew her down onto the plush Aubusson hearthrug. 'I have an idea. One that should satisfy us both.'

~ * ~

Justin leaned back on one elbow and unbuttoned the fall of his breeches with his other hand. As he released his cockstand then slowly stroked it, he watched Angelina's beautiful face. Her eyes widened at first but then she gave a shy smile. He hadn't wanted to shock her—he was well-endowed and Angelina was but a novice—so her reaction had him sighing with relief.

159

'You're so large,' she breathed as she watched him stroking himself. Her eyes sought his. 'Can I touch you? Like that?'

'Of course.'

She wrapped her elegant fingers around his shaft and squeezed gently. 'I never imagined... You feel so hot and hard. Like steel wrapped in silk.'

Justin groaned as she slid her hand from root to tip. If she kept this up it wouldn't be long before he exploded. But he had something else in mind.

Lying down, he reached for Angelina. 'Come and sit astride me, my lovely. Let us both find satisfaction.'

Curiosity dancing in her green eyes, she did as he directed, straddling his thighs, her warm wet furrow pressing against his throbbing shaft.

Arching his hips, he dragged his cock along her dew-slick folds, showing her what to do. 'Slide along my length,' he rasped. 'Take your pleasure from me and I shall take mine in return.'

Angelina needed no further encouragement. Leaning forward, she placed her hands beside his head then began to rhythmically glide back and forth. Justin grasped her hips and moved so his rigid cock rubbed against her peak, intensifying the pleasure for both of them. When he sucked one of her delicious nipples into his mouth, she shuddered and moaned before collapsing on top of him with a gentle sigh and he knew she'd found fulfilment again.

He wasn't far from release either. Lust pounding hot and hard through his veins, he ground his cock against Angelina's wet silken heat and on a ragged groan, he let go, his seed erupting between them in hot, powerful spurts.

Even though he hadn't come inside her, his climax had been sublime.

At length, Angelina pushed herself upright. Her tousled hair was a golden halo about her face. 'You think yourself a heartless rogue but I don't believe you are,' she whispered, a smile in her voice. Bending down, she gently kissed the tattoo on his sweat-slick chest then his lips.

Justin's heart swelled with unfamiliar emotion. Clearing his throat, he murmured, 'We shall wash and then sleep, my sweet.

Our bargain is settled. I am most satisfied.'

Her answering smile was as warm as a midsummer's day. 'As am I. Who'd have thought ruin could feel so wonderful.'

Some time later, as Angelina curled against him in his bed, he dropped a kiss on her temple. How odd that he, the infamous Tattooed Viscount, would envy the man she would undoubtedly wed one day.

~*~

Middleham House, Grosvenor Square. Two days later...

What a to-do!
Lady A.P. ruined by London's worst libertine, the Tattooed Viscount!
Will she be jilted by her affianced, Lord W?

Angelina stared at the scandal sheet that her father held in a shaking hand and willed herself not to cry. She had set this outrageous plan in motion so it was silly of her to be so upset.

'Is it true, Angelina?' her father demanded, his face crimson with rage. 'Did you really spend the night with Lord St Ives? Of all the miscreants...' He shook his head and sank into the chair behind his mahogany desk like a hot air balloon that had been deflated. 'I've already had word from Lord Wexford. He's furious and has called off the engagement. You'll be the death of me, child.'

Angelina swallowed past a hard lump in her throat and lifted her chin, determined to face the consequences of her actions with a brave face. Whilst part of her rejoiced at the thought she wouldn't have to marry Baron Wexford, her heart also ached to see her father so distressed. 'Yes. It is true, Papa. I'm so, so sorry to have disappointed you and Mama, but I just couldn't wed Lord Wexford. This seemed like the only way—'

The library door swung open and Angelina gasped for there, on the threshold, stood Justin, resplendent in formal morning dress with his black top hat in his gloved hands.

'What the devil?' exploded her father, leaping from his seat. 'What the hell are you doing here, St Ives? You're the scoundrel responsible for ruining my daughter. I'll have you thrown out of White's for this. Banned from The House of Lords. If I were a younger man, I'd call you out.'

Justin advanced into the room and bowed. 'Forgive me, Lord Middleham. But I beg to differ with your assessment of the situation. I will admit to compromising your daughter. But I have not ruined her.'

Lord Middleham thumped the desk with his fist. 'You damn well have. It's in every bloody scandal sheet on every corner. It's even in *The Times*!'

'Justin...' Angelina stepped forward, her heart pounding. 'What *are* you doing here?' Since she'd left his townhouse yesterday morning, she'd tried very hard not to think about him because whenever she did, she couldn't help but recall the bliss she'd found in his arms. He was the sort of man with whom she could easily fall in love. The sort of man she would love to marry.

But the Tattooed Viscount had also told her he wasn't the marrying kind. She dare not believe he'd suddenly transformed into a chivalrous knight-errant who'd rescue her from disgrace. She'd be wise to crush her hope before it had time to blossom.

'Lady Angelina.' Justin threw her a dazzling smile. 'You look lovely this morning.'

Before she could respond her father growled, 'Stop playing games and explain yourself, St Ives. What are you doing here?'

Justin met her father's hard gaze without flinching. 'If Lady Angelina is no longer betrothed, I wish to pay court with a view to marrying her, sir.'

Angelina's breath caught. 'Justin,' she whispered. Had she really just heard him correctly?

Justin cast his hat and gloves aside as he crossed the room. He took her trembling hands in his. 'My sweet Angelina,' he began, his topaz gaze warm with sincerity. 'I cannot stop thinking about you. And whenever I do, I cannot stop smiling. I'm smitten. Besotted. Falling headlong into love. You've brought my heart back to life and I would be truly honoured if you would consider my offer. '

She must be dreaming. 'Is... is that a proposal?'

Justin raised his hand and caressed her cheek. 'It is indeed, my angel. Marry me. Please say you'll be mine.'

Happiness bloomed inside Angelina's chest. How could she

refuse this wonderful man? 'Yes, Justin. My answer is yes. I believe I'm falling headlong into love with you too.'

Her father groaned. 'It's a *fait accompli*, isn't it?'

'I'm afraid so, Middleham,' said Justin over her head.

Angelina met her father's resigned gaze. 'Thank you, Papa,'

'As long as you're happy, my child.'

Justin captured her face between his hands. The light in his eyes warmed Angelina all the way to her toes. 'She will be. Always.' And then he sealed his promise with a kiss.

Want to try something a little sweeter?

Why not try our Little Gems Anthology?

Little Gems 2017

Onyx

http://romanceaustralia.com/shop/

Spicy Bites 2018

The theme for the 2018 Spicy Bites anthology will be…

Chains

For details of how to submit a story, please see Romance
Writers of Australia's website
http://romanceaustralia.com/contests/aspiring-
contests/spicy-bites/

About the Authors

Amy Rose Bennett
Amy Rose Bennett has always wanted to be a writer for as long as she can remember. An avid reader with a particular love for historical romance, it seemed only natural to write stories in her favourite genre. She has a passion for creating emotion-packed—and sometimes a little racy—stories set in the Georgian and Regency periods. Of course, her strong-willed heroines and rakish heroes always find their happily ever after. You can find out more about Amy's books by visiting her website: www.amyrosebennett.com

Nina Bridges
Nina Bridges is a British writer of romance and erotica. Her first novel, The Virgin's Gamble (under the pseudonym Gina Hollands), is due for release in late 2017 by The Wild Rose Press.
Serendipity is Nina's first erotic short story, and she is delighted it is appearing in the RWA's anthology.
When she's not writing, Nina can be found dancing – salsa, lindy hop, modern jive, rock 'n' roll – you name it, she'll boogie to it.
You can read more about her exploits at ginahollands.com and follow at facebook.com/ginahollands

Josephine Brierley
Salty hair, sandy toes, lips too often sipping white wine, Josephine Brierley is a Bali addict. Located on her favourite island, you can usually find her sitting at her favourite table—writing, people watching or gazing at the amazing ocean, with Chillidog her rescue pup, usually at her feet.
Her romantic stories will entice you with steamy, sexy and fun tales, filled with real-life sagas and characters that you can't help fall in love with.
For more author news and information on her island life, go to http://www.josephinebrierleyauthor.com

Kristine Charles

Kristine Charles loves telling sexy tales, exploring relationships between complex women and the strong men who love them, then working out just how much pain to inflict, or not inflict, before giving her characters their HEA (or, at least, their HFN). She writes, and reads, to escape into other worlds where coffee (and red wine) is abundant, designer shoes and handbags are cheap, chocolate has no calories and men *always* put the toilet seat down. Find her at <u>wordsbykristinecharles.com</u> or tweet her @wordsbykc.

Audrey Fraser

Audrey is a long-time fan of romance stories and adventure films, currently living in North Queensland with a plethora of characters that may (or not) turn up in a book someday. She has an alarmingly large library but has no plans to stop buying and reading interesting books. Audrey has travelled extensively with varying degrees of satisfaction and performed onstage solo and with a choir. Collecting experiences is her favourite hobby and learning something new is always valued. Audrey demands a happy and enjoyable ending in all her stories and if something explodes, all the better.

Caitlyn Lynch

Caitlyn Lynch is an Australian mother of two who has always enjoyed reading and writing romantic fiction. Happily married to her very own tall, dark and handsome for 14 years and counting, she draws on a rich imagination to create new scenarios for her steamy contemporary romances.

She has lately started Shenanigans Press, dedicated to helping first-time authors gain experience in the world of self-publishing through a series of short story anthologies.

You can find her at her website caitlynlynch.com, or on Facebook, Twitter and Tumblr.

Annabelle McInnes

The Refuge Trilogy is poignant to Annabelle's personal story. From the age of sixteen, she lived in a Youth Refuge while she remained committed to her education. Her experiences are the foundations that drive her stories and her characters. They are the people that civilisation left behind and yet they still fight for their freedoms, have courage in the face of adversity and aspire for greatness.

Did you love Without Refuge? True Refuge, book one in the Refuge Trilogy will be published in September 2017.

Follow Annabelle on Twitter @akmcinnes, Instagram @annabellemcinnes and Facebook @authorannabellemcinnes. Sign up to her newsletter at www.annabellemcinnes.com

Nardia Sheriff

Growing up, Nardia Sheriff always wanted to be a writer. Well, that and a lawyer in the Navy; thank you, Tom Cruise. Alas, a fear of gigantic boats and rough seas saw her choose marketing over law, but her childhood dream of being an author never faded. Currently writing her first novel, Nardia is taking time out from the rat race to travel around the country in a caravan with her two favourite little people and her truck-driving hubby. Nardia blogs about her travels and hangs out in all cool places online under @nardiasheriff and @alifelikeours.

Wren St Clair

Wren St Claire has wanted to write since she was 12 years old and fell in love with her mother's Georgette Heyer collection. But it took longer to realise the dream of writing than she anticipated. Wren writes an eclectic mix of story types from hotter than hell contemporaries, to sweet Regencies, and fantasy adventure stories of Ancient Egypt. She holds a Masters in Egyptology and used to lead tours to Egypt before the revolution. She lives in Brisbane with her husband, two ancient miniature schnauzers and a mad Bengal cat. Check out her very hot MMF Romance It's Impossible: Loving one is hard, loving two is even harder. www.wrenstclaire.com

Kerrie Starbuck

Kerrie Starbuck started reading her mother's Mills & Boon books in high school and never really stopped. Some time ago, she decided she should write one. Since then she's won several contests but is still waiting for that elusive contract. Nevertheless, she persists. One day (before she's tragically crushed to death by her To Be Read pile), she would like to see her own name on the cover of a full-length romance novel. She can often be found on Twitter under the name @KL_Starbuck, one-clicking Amazon book links from all her favourite authors.

Lee-Ann Wallace

Lee-Ann Wallace wants to live in a world where washing folds itself, coffee's good for you, and dreams come true (at least the good ones).

When she's not tapping away at her computer working on her next Erotic Romance story, you can find her daydreaming about her next tattoo, watching action movies with her family, and practicing self-control, so she doesn't one click every book on Amazon.

Find out more about Lee-Ann's current releases and what she's working on now at www.leeannwallace.com